Watch Me Want Me

by

Honey McGregor

Cover designed by Honey McGregor

This book is a work of fiction. Names, characters, places, and incidents either are products of the author's imagination or are used fictitiously. Any resemblance to actual persons, living or dead, events, or locales is entirely coincidental.

Honey McGregor

www.honeymcgregor.blogspot.com
www.facebook.com/honeymcgregorauthor

Published by Honey McGregor

Also by Honey McGregor
Private Pleasures: The Collection
Dina Island

Table of Contents

NOW - ADDICTION

Matt turned the key in the front door, impatiently, and rushed straight to his laptop. His heart was already beating more rapidly and his mouth felt dry. He just wanted to check if she was there... waiting for him... and ready for him...

Savanna showered quickly and began to apply lotion to her smooth skin, wondering which clothing to wear for the evening ahead. Would he visit her again tonight? So far, he'd starred her six times, not a lot, admittedly, but as she was new to it all it still felt quite good. She wondered who he was...

Nothing. She wasn't online yet. His heart sank. He had to get a grip, he told himself. Be cool, go take a shower, grab a beer, maybe check back later...

She decided on a set of sheer white lingerie, over the knee socks, a tiny flared skirt in a plaid fabric, and a white blouse in thin cotton. Yes, she smiled approvingly at her reflection, the school girl look, very nice. Okay, shoes though... what would work with the outfit?

'Has anyone got a pair of mary janes in a six? Preferably with a heel?' A few faces looked up, at her enquiry, some of the girls getting ready to start, some to leave. Silently, Maria handed her the pair she'd just taken off, smiling and giving her a wink as she took in her outfit. 'You make a very cute and sexy school girl, Savanna.'

'Honestly mate, not tonight, I'm knackered.' Matt's protest fell on deaf ears as his best friend, Sam, shouldered his way past him and into his house.

Sam opened two beers and handed one to Matt, before taking a long swig from his own bottle. 'It's been almost three months, mate, you need to start getting out a bit. It's not healthy you staying in on your own every night, crying yourself to sleep. Come on, let's get down to the pub, a few of the others'll be there.'

Matt glanced hopelessly at his laptop, a glance that Sam noticed straightaway. 'Oh no you don't, what's so important on there that you'd rather stay in than come down the pub with your mates?'

Sam moved to Matt's laptop as Matt roughly pushed past him to close the lid. 'Whoa, take it easy!' he exclaimed, moving out of Matt's way.

Sam put his hands up, *Watch Me Want Me*, are you serious? So that's why we never see you anymore! I sent that to you for a laugh, after Nicky said her friend was on it, I didn't expect you to get addicted!'

Matt felt embarrassed. 'Of course I'm not addicted. The girls are hot, that's all, can't blame a bloke for checking them out!' Come on, let's go down the pub then. Matt steered Sam out of the house, anything to stop him prying further into his online activities.

With her make-up all done it was just the wig that was left. She watched in amazement, as she did every time, at the complete change in her appearance once she was wearing the wig. The platinum blonde bob was in stark contrast to her naturally dark brows and eyes, adding to the overall sexy look. She'd always had a hankering to try out the colour, she'd just never been brave enough until now. Now that she was playing a role, that is...

She took her props into her room and set them out on the bed, her laptop, a few books, a satchel containing a bag of sweets and a ruler, and finally, a magazine. Not just any magazine, *See-Through* was for adults only and she found that it helped get her in the mood, as well as her viewers, when she let them catch a glimpse of what she was looking at...

She checked her webcams from her laptop and stretched out on her stomach on the bed, tightening and pushing up her buttocks so that they swelled up invitingly under her short skirt. Sometimes she amazed herself at how quickly she'd got used to all this, and maybe more worryingly, how quickly she'd begun to enjoy it... She clicked *live*.

Matt had forgotten how good it felt to be out with the lads, to get pissed and have a laugh. Sam had been right, it was exactly what he needed. He lost count of how many beers they consumed, knowing he'd regret it the next day, but not caring, at least it was the weekend. The kebab on the way home was the perfect ending to the evening and it was only as he unlocked his door that he realised he hadn't thought of her for a while...

It had been a slow evening and even though she'd had a good number of viewers they'd only stayed for a minute or two each time. She'd been starred by a couple of fans, as they called them, and had a chat with one of them, but it wasn't him...

She wondered who he was, what he looked like, was he married? Old? Young? He could be anyone and anything, a though that both scared her and thrilled her at the same time. She popped a sweet into her mouth, curling her tongue around it teasingly as she looked at the camera.

There'd been no special requests tonight so she'd not earned anything extra, but before she finished her session, she decided to give her last two viewers a little treat. She rolled onto her back and bent her knees in the air, spreading her legs slightly. Angling herself towards the camera, she let her fingers pull teasingly on the top of her panties, closing her eyes and opening her mouth a little.

The gentle ping on her laptop told her that she had another viewer and she rolled over to see who it was. Maybe it was him... please let it be him...

Matt fumbled on his laptop, signing in quickly and clicking on Savanna's photo. She was live! He sat down as he clicked on *watch live*, his eyes glued to the screen, and he watched her roll over to check her screen. She looked up and smiled, giving him a little wave.

He waved back, knowing that she couldn't see him, feeling a little silly. She looked gorgeous, sweet and sexy in her school girl outfit. He could feel his cock hardening immediately. Whatever he'd said to Sam, he knew that he was becoming seriously addicted, not to the site but to her...

She clicked on *personal chat* and typed 'Hello, Action Man, I missed you this evening.' Her screen pinged but it wasn't from him, it was a credit from viewer two. Reading the request, she smiled as she positioned herself up on her knees. She leaned forward exaggeratedly to reveal her panty clad bottom as she looked for something inside her satchel.

Matt felt a stab of jealousy as the screen went dark and the *private request in progress* message appeared on his screen. Fuck! What was she doing? What had some bastard asked her to do? Frantically he clicked on *private request*, he'd ask her to do something for him, anything, to stop the other guy from watching her.

She held the ruler in the air and brought it down on her panty clad buttocks. If viewer two wanted her to be punished for being a naughty girl, who was she to deny him? It was a pretty harmless request, she thought, as she pushed her bottom up higher and continued to take her self-inflicted punishment.

Your credit is about to expire ACTION MAN, please recharge your account to continue. Matt stared at his screen in disbelief. How could that be? He'd put £100 on only the other day, surely he hadn't spent it already? He looked around for his wallet but realised that he must have put it down in the bedroom. Fuck, again.

She switched back to *live* and looked hopefully at her screen, but he'd gone. Disappointment washed over her, she'd been so looking forward to chatting with him. Suddenly she wanted to go too. Home... or what passed as home these days... She clicked *end* and closed her laptop, checking that the winking lights on the webcams had gone off.

He entered his card number and, this time, recklessly added £200 to his account. Clicking on her name he decided he'd finally ask her to go further this time. Why should the other viewers have all the fun? He wasn't a perv, he wouldn't get her to do anything demeaning, just maybe give him a glimpse of what was underneath that cute little schoolgirl outfit. He clicked her name twice more before he realised that she was offline. Fuck.

Honey McGregor

THEN - GOING WRONG

Could silence be deafening? When did it become so hard to find something to say? Tanya uncurled herself from her position on the sofa and stood up. 'D'you want something to eat then?' she asked Matt, already heading for the kitchen.

Irritation rose as she realised that he hadn't heard her, or hadn't bothered to reply more likely. She opened the fridge, looking for inspiration. Cold chicken, half a pizza... nothing interesting. She took out the leftover pizza and switched the oven on, heading back to the lounge. 'Pizza alright?'

'What?' Matt looked up from his tablet, the TV competing with her as she asked him again.

'I said, is pizza alright, didn't you hear me?'

'Sorry, babe, yeah, pizza's fine.' He looked back at his tablet, grinning at something, Facebook probably.

Tanya sighed. 'I'm going to take a shower, while the oven heats up, then.' Not waiting for his reply, and not really expecting one, she went upstairs and into their bedroom, unbuttoning her shirt as she walked.

Standing under the hot shower, she let her thoughts drift as she soaped her body. There would've been a time when Matt would have got up, with a cheeky grin on his face, and chased her to the shower, stripping off and getting in with her.

She closed her eyes and tried to remember what his hands on her body had felt like. Slowly she ran her hands over her soapy body, imagining it was him. Her nipples hardened, as soon as her touch stroked over them, and she felt a familiar pull further down.

Matt leaned back on the couch, listening for the sound of the shower to start. Satisfied, he clicked on the link Sam had sent him and, with an almost furtive feel, began to scroll. Fuck, these girls were hot. What was it Sam had said? Nicky was on it? No way, that wasn't it, her friend was, that's right. How the hell did Sam's sister have a mate who worked on a sex site? Wondering which one she was, he continued to scroll.

The combination of the warm evening, the hot shower and her nakedness was making her feel so bloody horny. She touched herself between her legs, sliding her fingers gently over her swelling clit and feeling a jolt as her body responded hungrily. With one hand gently stroking her nipples, she began to masturbate with the other, leaning back against the tiled wall and pushing her pelvis forward as her fingers moved faster.

Matt listened for the shower. It was still running, what the hell was Tanya doing in there? He paused over the photo of *Alexa*, and, with a final glance towards the lounge door, clicked on it to view the larger image. Shit! Talk about gorgeous! Tall and slim with perfect breasts, Alexa's hair fell in waves over her shoulders, skimming her large nipples as they jutted teasingly above some kind of lacy bodice. Her hands played with the waistband of her short skirt, pulling it down to give a tantalising glimpse of lace panties...

She shoved her fingers inside herself as her movements became almost involuntary, urgently moving them in and out and spreading her silky juices over her straining clit. A small moan escaped her as she suddenly started coming, her body taking on its own shuddering jolts as her orgasm took over completely.

With a small gasp, she slumped against the tiles, feeling weakness take over her legs. She let the water run over her body as she rinsed herself, washing away the evidence of her pleasure, before turning the taps off and stepping out of the shower.

His cock was hard and pushing against his loose shorts. Hell, it was virtually asking him to touch it. Tentatively he reached inside his shorts, one ear still on the running shower upstairs. Alexa's eyes smiled provocatively into his as he grasped his penis, running his hand over the tip to spread his leaking cum. He moved faster, his eyes raking over her gorgeous breasts and down to her skirt, being pushed down just for him.

He was aware of the shower turning off just as he came, trying not to make any noise. His cum spilled into and through his fingers, as he grasped his cock, and he reached for some tissues.

'You all done? Think I'll jump in now then.' Matt leaned against the doorframe, taking in his girlfriend's naked body as she quickly pulled on panties and reached for her t-shirt.

Stupid! She actually felt guilty, as if she'd done something bad behind Matt's back, cheated on him or something. She pulled her shorts on and smiled at him. 'I'll go and pop the pizza in the oven, it should be ready by the time you've showered.'

Matt washed off the remains of his masturbating under the hot shower, feeling slightly guilty. He wondered what Tanya would think of him wanking off to some chick on the internet. Well, it wasn't real, was it? It wasn't as if he was actually *cheating* on her with someone...

'Want some wine, babe?' The pizza was out of the oven and smelt good. He fetched two glasses and picked up the bottle of red, which had been sitting on the counter for a few days. Suddenly he wanted to make his girlfriend feel good. 'You look nice, new top?'

Tanya laughed, 'New? I've had this for about a year, but thanks!' She turned back to the cupboard and reached for the plates, but she had a little smile on ier face. Suddenly she yearned for the comfortable and happy intimacy of their earlier days together. 'Shall we sit outside? It's such a lovely evening.'

Matt paused with the wine bottle, 'Er, yeah, okay, why not? I'll take the wine out then.' He set the glasses down on their outdoor table and opened the wine, pouring their drinks as Tanya appeared with the plates of pizza and some paper serviettes.

'This is nice.' Tanya smiled at him as they ate their pizza in the warm air of the summer's evening. 'I can't remember when we last did this can you?' Matt nodded, his mouth full, and reached a hand across to squeeze hers. They smiled at each other and Tanya reached for the bottle to top them up.

They finished their food and leaned back, both with their own thoughts, as they drank their wine.

Tanya stretched her legs out in front of her, feeling languid, and a little sexy, if she was honest - the after effects of her moment of self-pleasure in the shower, she supposed. She glanced sideways at Matt to see if he was looking at her, but he was gazing down into his glass. Maybe he just didn't fancy her any more. But he had told her she looked nice earlier. Maybe she just needed to make more effort.

Matt's thoughts were on Alexa again. He'd only looked at her free photos and they were hot enough. He wondered what else she revealed if you paid for more. The *live* button had been winking on her profile, what did that mean then? He looked over at Tanya but could only think of Alexa. 'Shall we watch a movie?'

Tanya sighed inwardly, what had she been hoping for anyway? That they'd suddenly jump each other just because they'd sat outside eating pizza and drinking wine? 'Yeah, sure, you find something, I'll clear the plates.'

Bruce Willis's voice nudged its way into her consciousness and she realised that she hadn't been watching. They'd watched these Die Hard movies before, more than once, they were more Matt's thing than hers, if she was honest.

Matt clocked Tanya stir herself and knew that she'd drifted off from the movie. If he was honest, he'd known she wouldn't really be into it, that she'd probably decide to head off to bed before him. He glanced towards his tablet, still switched off from earlier, and thought about Alexa again...

Leaning back into the cushions Tanya thought about how she'd felt earlier, in the shower. With surprise she realised that she was feeling horny again, it must be the bloody weather. Well, she acknowledged to herself, probably more to do with total sexual frustration, they hadn't touched each other for weeks, no wonder she was horny. She glanced at Matt but his eyes were glued to the TV screen. She thought about the cool cotton bed sheets on their bed and imagined slipping naked between them... 'I'll think I'll go to bed, are you going to carry on watching?'

'Yeah, d'you mind? Night, babe.' Matt gave her arm a rub, as she stood up, and watched her leave the lounge. He listened as she fetched water from the fridge and headed upstairs, the familiar sounds of her night time rituals reaching his ears. Satisfied that she wasn't coming back downstairs again he reached for his tablet.

Stupid, she felt kind of excited at the thought of getting naked into bed, without Matt! What was wrong with her? Pretty obvious, if she really thought about it, she was horny, and still feeling floaty from having pleasured herself in the shower earlier. Nothing ever happened between them in bed anymore, so why not just give herself some pleasure of her own again?

He quickly scrolled through, looking for Alexa. There she was, and she was still live! He clicked on the *watch live* button and read the details in the pop-up window. Damn, he needed to register and pay before he could watch any more. But his wallet was upstairs...

Tanya lay between the cool sheets, just the feel of the crisp cotton on her nipples filling her with desire. God, she really *was* feeling horny if that was all it took. She thought about Matt, picturing him naked in bed with her, his hands reaching for her...

No, he wouldn't risk it, not now, plenty of time for that. He'd have a look at a few of the other girls instead, his cock hardening in anticipation at the thought...

Matt wasn't doing it for her, no surprise there. She let her mind wander, picturing different guys in her mind. Simon, at work, was pretty hot, in a suit and tie kind of way... She imagined them in the staff kitchenette, both staying late. No, picturing someone she knew didn't work. She imagined a faceless stranger instead, her hand moving down over her body as she arched herself towards her fingers...

Star gazed back at him, as he pulled his shorts down to release his penis. It sprang out and he grasped it, slowly moving his hand up and down as he continued to take in Star's bush, showing beneath her tiny, tight, white dress...

Her body responded hungrily to her touch, her thighs parting for her hand to reach between them. The tips of her fingers gently skimmed over her swollen labia, as they parted to allow her budding arousal to push through between them. The secrecy of what she was doing, with Matt just downstairs, added to her heat. But it was the faceless stranger's fingers touching her that made her gasp, as she began to tease herself with her fingers, slipping them inside to coat them in her own wet desire.

He imagined Star slowly lifting her dress up, to reveal her exposed bush. She wasn't wearing any panties, so fucking hot. He grasped his cock harder, imagining her spreading her legs apart to show him her wet pussy. His hand moved faster as he pictured her sitting on him, his cock slipping inside her. He fucked her hard, hearing her gasps of pleasure, before realising they were his gasps as he came, his spasms shooting his creamy cum out over his hand and onto his thigh.

Frantically she touched her nipples with her one hand, as her other hand moved faster, in and out, wetness beginning to ooze out as she parted her legs still further. Her pelvis strained upwards as she plunged two fingers inside herself, pushing hard against her clit, so that she groaned out loud as she came. Her orgasm was intense and when, finally, her hips lowered again, she slumped into the sheets, her fingers still resting between her legs as she drifted off to sleep.

Honey McGregor

NOW - PRIVATE REQUEST

She was feeling quite tired, it had been a long day and the thought of working this evening wasn't holding much appeal if she was honest. But then she thought about him, she didn't want to disappoint him and she did enjoy their chats... and she enjoyed the thrill of knowing he enjoyed watching her even more...

Matt's working day was over and he was mulling over whether to pick up a curry on the way home or whether he had anything at home to cook himself. The curry won easily and he headed for the Indian restaurant near his house.

As she showered, she thought about how weird her life was now. Not that long ago they'd been a couple, living together, planning their future together. Yeah, sure, life had got a little boring, they'd got set in their ways, but didn't that happen to all couples after a few years? How had they let it get so bad that they'd actually separated, albeit temporarily, supposedly? She wondered what he was doing right at this moment...

The curry had gone down a treat and, freshly showered, beer in hand, Matt settled himself at his laptop. Weird, it was starting to feel like getting ready for a date each time he logged on now. She couldn't see him, but he still kind of imagined that she could.

Savanna checked her full-length reflection in the mirror as she chatted to some of the girls before they went into their rooms. She'd gone for the all-black lace look, from the balconette bra and thong, to the suspender belt and stockings and just the act of wearing it was making her feel pretty sexy. Over her lingerie she was wearing a tight little black t-shirt with a black mini skirt and the pole dancing heels finished off the look to perfection.

Matt clicked through on his laptop and signed in to *Watch Me Want Me* (visit the accompanying webpage at www.watchmewantme.blogspot.com), his eyes already scanning for her name. She wasn't live and he felt disappointed. Maybe she wasn't on tonight? Should he wait or check out some of the other girls? Or would he feel like he was cheating on her? He laughed to himself. Idiot. Cheating on a girl on a sex site. His eyes fell on a lone earring in a dish on the table. It was Tanya's, if he was cheating on anyone it was her. But it wasn't really cheating, was it? And they *were* separated...

Savanna surveyed her room before going *live*. She threw a white cover over the bed and angled the couch more in front of one of the cameras. She poured herself a glass of wine and, feeling quite in character, she went *live*. Her eyes scanned the screen on her laptop, noting how many viewers lit up at the top of the screen. She had quite a following now, she thought, feeling an amused pride.

Oh God, she was *live*! Quickly he clicked on her photo and his screen revealed the beautiful sight of Savanna, seated on a couch, her legs crossed, and the sexiest pair of shoes he'd ever seen adorning her feet. His eyes drank her in, noting the bare flesh at the top of her stockings, the hint of suspender straps before they disappeared under her little skirt.

He was here! She smiled up at the webcam and re-crossed her legs, giving him a brief glimpse of the tops of her thighs. 'Hi, Action Man, I've missed you'.

Matt typed quickly, a smile on his face. 'Hi, Savanna, I've missed you too! You look bloody sexy tonight, is that for me?' He watched her smile as she read his message. She looked up at him and nodded, her scarlet painted lips giving him a sexy pout.

'What have you been up to today?' She wanted to keep him chatting, he was good fun and always made her feel good, without feeling dirty. Not like some of the other guys. Talking of which, here was Horny Boy with a message. She read it, trying to keep her smile on her face. 'I want to bend you over and fuck you from behind.' She hoped he wasn't going to private request her, God knows what he'd ask for...

'Just another day in the office, thinking of you... How was your day?' He really wanted to know, she intrigued him. There was something different about her, not the jaded look that some of the other girls had. He wondered what she looked like without all her make-up on, and without her hair covering part of her face.

Normally they'd play along with the fantasy to their viewers, when they chatted to them. Talk about how they'd spent the day masturbating in the bath, thinking about whoever it was, saying they were wet already, just from seeing the name come up. Stuff like that. But with Action Man it was different, she sensed some kind of loneliness from him, and it seemed like he really did care...

'Oh, it was ok, my day job, you know, nothing exciting, same old same old.'

Same old same old. Tanya always used that expression. 'What d'you do in your day job, Savanna? Tell me more!' He wondered if she would, she didn't give much away...

Careful. Never give too much away they'd been warned. You never knew which of these guys might turn out to be a sicko. Not that she thought Action Man was, but best to be safe and tell a white lie here and there. 'Oh, I just work in a restaurant, nothing glamourous, a bit of waitressing and behind the bar.'

She worked in a restaurant! Worked behind the bar too. That meant he'd be able to actually see her for real, if he knew where it was. 'Anywhere I know?' Stupid question. She didn't know where he lived and he had no idea where she actually was! She could be anywhere. But no, hold on, Sam's sister's mate worked for the sex site, so it must be fairly local...

'Oh, that would be telling...' She looked up and winked. 'Hold on.' She had a private request from Horny Man, dammit. Oh, how bloody predictable, he wanted to see her touch herself through her panties and make herself come, while he looked at her from behind. She clicked the privacy button for Horny Man and turned round on the couch, facing her bottom towards the camera.

Matt felt the usual frustration when Savanna's screen went dark. Each time it happened his jealousy grew. He wished he knew what she was doing for some other guy perving over her. He tapped his fingers on the table, downed his beer and went and fetched another, taking a large gulp as he sat down. He pictured her in her black outfit with her stockings leading up to her thighs, feeling his cock heavy and hard as it began to swell.

She kneeled, leaning forward slightly, with her bottom up in the air, looking back at the camera through half-closed eyes. She still wasn't sure how she felt about doing this. Part of her felt too dirty, if she was honest, but the other part felt a distinct thrill. The worst thing was not knowing who the guy was. Was he some revolting, greasy old man who never washed, sitting there in his dirty underpants, getting his rocks off? No, don't think like that, think of Action Man, imagine it's him...

Slowly she stroked her fingers over herself, through the lacy thong, where it disappeared down between her legs. She rubbed her fingers in circles and could feel the responding swelling as her pleasure grew. Wetness started to seep through the sheer lace and she parted her legs still further, her eyes closed now. Her fingers moved faster and she could feel the heat rising in her body as she neared her orgasm. That was enough, never go too far, you've set limits. She eased the pressure off and pretended to come with a few gasps and a couple of pushes of her pelvis. She sank back onto the couch cushions and opened her eyes, giving a smile up to the camera.

'Sorry about that.' She was back! 'Tell me more about yourself, Action Man.' He wondered what to tell her. There wasn't much to tell really.

'Oh, I'm just a sad, lonely guy.' He paused. 'But not so sad when I look at you! You already know about my boring job in shipping. I'm single, haven't found the one, I suppose.' Guilt flashed through him. Well, he could hardly say he was on a temporary separation from his girlfriend could he? And was it really temporary? It had been a few months now.

'I'm sorry you're sad and lonely. Can I do anything to make you feel better?' She was pushing him, she knew, but he'd never gone so far as to private request her yet. Her faux orgasm earlier, for Horny Man, had left her feeling a little hot and she wouldn't mind doing something for Action Man. She actually totally wanted to...

Matt hesitated. He knew if he asked for a private request he'd be taking things further. So far, he'd just watched her and chatted to her. The things she did while she was *live* were fairly innocent, in the scheme of things. He'd

13

watched her flash her underwear as she'd uncrossed her legs, watched her skirt ride up as she'd lain on the bed in various poses. He'd held his breath as she'd leaned over to the camera, to give a view of her breasts as they swelled out of her bra. What could he ask her for that wouldn't be demeaning? He didn't want her to think he was a sicko. He started to type a reply.

Oh, bless him! He was so sweet. And decent. He didn't want to ask her to do anything that made her feel dirty. He didn't even know what he *could* ask her to do. Could she give him some suggestions maybe? Thinking quickly, she smiled as she replied.

Matt read Savanna's reply, feeling like a little boy. She could touch herself if he wanted, maybe her breasts, or somewhere else if he wanted? She could do a striptease, but outer clothes only. She didn't *get naked* for her requests. She could play with herself... He only had to ask...

Taking a deep breath, Matt typed with trembling fingers. 'I'd love to see you in your underwear, lying on the bed. I want to imagine touching you... Tell me it's okay and I'll private request you.'

Her reply came back. 'It's ok, Action Man.'

Her other viewers' lights went off when she hit *private request* so she knew there was no-one waiting for her to come back on right now. She stood in front of the camera and gazed into it as she slowly lifted her t-shirt up and over her head.

Matt watched, entranced, as Savanna's breasts were revealed, barely covered in the lace bra. Her nipples could just be seen peeping above the lace edge of the half-cup bra. His cock was hard as rock and he stood up, pulling his shorts off so that he was wearing only his boxer shorts.

Next, she undid her skirt and let it fall to the ground, exposing her stocking clad legs. She climbed onto the bed and laid back, gazing up at the camera. She felt hot and sexy and she parted her legs a little, drawing her knees up slightly so that she could touch herself.

Fuck, she was hot! Matt stared at his computer screen, watching Savanna's hand as it reached between her legs, her other hand moving to stroke over her breasts. As she touched her nipples, he saw them tighten and poke through the lace, pushing up slightly higher so that they almost escaped the top, lacy edge of her bra.

His hand was on his cock, his juices already leaking out of the tip, and he began to run his hand up and down along its length, spreading the wetness so that his hand glided easily. He felt like he was going to explode, she was so fucking beautiful. He imagined walking into the room, standing in front of her as she laid back on the bed, gently easing her legs further apart....

Savanna started to touch herself through her panties, feeling a surge of arousal as she became immediately wet. She was feeling really fucking horny now. She imagined that he was here, in the room, his hand reaching forward to

14

touch her between her legs. She rubbed her fingers over herself and pushed her mound up, wanting to slip her fingers inside, whilst knowing that she didn't usually offer that. But she was losing control...

Matt's hand was moving fast now, up and down, slicking over his cum-leaking penis as he watched Savanna writhe on the bed. This was real. She wasn't acting. He could see the dark, glistening, patch on her panties where she was wet, could see her fingers probing herself, trying to go inside... He imagined his fingers touching her pussy, feeling her wetness as it slicked over her pubic hairs. He pictured his fingers pulling her panties aside and slipping inside her, cupping his hand tightly around his cock for more pleasure.

Casting care aside she slipped her panties to one side and slid her fingers over her clit, circling it and then plunging them inside with a gasp. It felt so good, she began to move faster, her hips pushing up towards her hand as she slipped her wet fingers over her clit and back inside. She was straining upwards now, nearing orgasm, and she moved her fingers in and out frantically, her eyes still on the camera, and on Action Man...

Fuck! Matt lost control, coming with a groan, his body almost convulsing as his sperm shot out over his hand. Still he moved his hand up and down his cock a few more times as he slowly shuddered to a finish. His eyes were glued on Savanna's pussy as she pushed upwards one last time and then, her eyes closing, orgasmed in front of him. She looked so beautiful, as she slowly removed her wet fingers from between her legs, her swollen lips wide open showing him where they'd both just been.

The screen went dark for a couple of minutes and then his laptop pinged as she appeared back on the screen. 'Did you like that?'

'Oh my God, I loved it!' Matt leaned back in his chair. 'Did you like it too?' He took in her flushed face and shy smile, knowing that she'd enjoyed it as much as him.

'I did! But don't tell anyone, it's our secret! I don't usually do that... But I have to go now, Action Man, I really do, sorry. Chat soon xx'

She signed off, suddenly feeling overcome with the enormity of what she'd just done, of what they'd *both* done. She needed to be alone, felt embarrassed, wanted time to think through what just happened.

'Bye, Savanna, when are you next on?' But she was gone.

Honey McGregor

THEN - MISUNDERSTANDINGS AND MASTURBATIONS

Matt watched Tanya walk in the door, noting how miserable she looked. 'Alright babe, long day?'

Tanya dropped her bag on the kitchen counter before heading upstairs. Work had been a nightmare today, her boss had been in a bad mood, they were behind on their deadlines and she'd had to stay late. But that hadn't stopped her boss from just texting her to complain about something else. She was so tired she couldn't think straight, she just wanted to fall into bed.

'Matt!' She sounded pissed off. 'You could have made the bed, like I asked you! And picked up your dirty clothes and your wet towel!'

Matt groaned inwardly, here we go again. He never did anything right these days. Why was it his job anyway? When was that decided? He got up and went upstairs. 'D'you have to have a go at me as soon as you get in? That is, after you ignored me when I spoke to you?'

'You never spoke to me! I, however, did text you to ask you to make up the bed and get the washing out of the machine. But that was obviously too much to ask when I'm working late.'

Shit! Matt looked around for his mobile, patting his pockets when he couldn't see it lying anywhere. He must have left it in the car. He picked up his keys and went to retrieve his phone, reading her message as he walked back into the house.

'Sorry, babe, you're right, I didn't see your text, left my phone in the car. I know, I know, *again*... I'll do the bed now then sort out the washing. But Tans, you did ignore me when you walked in, it works both ways you know.'

She took a breath, 'Sorry, I was totally distracted, problems at work, I probably just didn't hear you.'

Having attempted apologies they both got busy, he with domestic chores, she with a quick shower. They reconvened in the kitchen where the usual question arose. What's for dinner? The simple answer was nothing, the remedy was a quick call for Chinese and time to find a movie to watch.

Tanya felt totally miserable, her day had been shit, and Matt hadn't even asked her about it, even when she told him she'd had problems at work.

Matt felt deflated, he'd had a good day at work, been told he might be in line for a promotion. But Tanya never asked him about his day and now that they'd already had the usual bickering that seemed to be part of every evening, he didn't feel like telling her.

Tanya poured herself a glass of wine, holding the bottle out to Matt enquiringly. 'No, I'll grab a beer thanks.' The doorbell rang and he went to pay for the food while she got plates out.

The movie credits came up and Matt stood up, yawning. 'I'm pretty knackered, think I'll hit the sack.'

Tanya watched him leave the lounge and then resignedly picked up the dirty plates from the coffee table. Typical, he hadn't even noticed they were still there. She put them in the dishwasher and switched on her laptop. She'd better have a look at the files her boss had sent through.

Matt walked through to get some water. 'You're working? Bit late, isn't it?'

She gave him a smile, 'I know, but Mark'll kill me if I don't go through this stuff before tomorrow. It should only take me an hour or two hopefully. I'll be up after that'

Matt picked up his tablet on the way out, as he called out goodnight. Maybe he'd have a little look online...

He dropped his clothes on the chair and got into bed, naked, reaching for his tablet and logging onto *Watch Me Want Me*. Tanya might not be interested in making him feel good but these chicks did the job pretty well instead.

He scrolled through, amazed at how many hot chicks there were on the site. So far, he'd only checked out the free photos, hadn't taken the next step of registering and buying credit. His fingers hesitated, he glanced at the bedroom door, then quickly began to type.

He needed a user name, well yeah, that was obvious. His mind cast around for inspiration and he tried a couple of options that were already taken before being accepted as *Action Man*. Yeah, he kind of liked that. Well now he'd registered he may as well buy a little credit, just so he could have a look...

Shit! Fuck me! This was a whole new world, well, he'd looked at plenty of porn before, but this was different. These girls were shit hot and sitting in their own rooms, on camera. Some rooms were bedrooms, others living rooms and one was even decked out like a bar, the girl in question sitting up on a bar stool with a glass of wine.

As he stared at *Peaches* she shifted slightly on the stool, uncrossing her long legs and re-crossing them as she smiled straight at him. Matt felt his cock harden under the duvet at the sight of her lace top hold-ups and the glimpse of lace panties.

'Did you like that, Action Man?' The question appeared on the right of his screen. Matt froze. She couldn't see him! He felt stupid. Of course she couldn't, his user name must come up somewhere. He looked more closely, there was a laptop on the bar beside her which she glanced at.

Should he reply? Nothing wrong he supposed, it was just a laugh. 'Very nice, Peaches...' He waited to see what she'd do next.

'What else would you like to see? I'm open to private requests... I just have a few rules...'

He read the rules which appeared on his screen, well, all two of them. She wouldn't penetrate herself with anything other than the dildos she had on display and she never showed her anus. Everything else was okay.

Phew. This girl was pretty generous with her offerings. What the hell did other blokes ask her to do? And how much did a private request cost? He scanned the information about private requests and typed a message quickly, feeling turned on.

Peaches gave him another of her seductive smiles as she stood up and began to unbutton her blouse. Her large breasts bounced out as she removed the blouse, the flimsy bra barely supporting them. Matt watched, mesmerised, his hand unconsciously holding his cock which was rock hard and aching with desire.

She turned around as she undid her skirt, letting it drop to the floor and stepping out of it in her high heels. Sitting back on the stool, she kept her legs apart and began to gently writhe around, giving him beautiful glimpses of her panties where they covered her bush and disappeared between her thighs.

Matt kept his eyes locked on Peaches as she looked straight at him, one of her hands now touching her nipples through the flimsy fabric of her bra. His hand moved fast as he bought himself closer to release, holding back just enough until she removed her bra.

He glanced at the door, then back at his screen, not wanting to miss a moment of this. He was close to coming and, as her hand stroked over her naked breasts he watched her nipples grow and harden. Fuck! She slipped her other hand between her legs and began to touch herself, but Matt ejaculated, unable to hold it any longer.

He gasped quietly, looking at the bedroom door, listening for any sounds of Tanya, but all was quiet downstairs. His tablet pinged. 'Was that good, honey?' Good? It was fucking excellent!

'It was great, Peaches!' He signed off quickly, wanting to clean up in the bathroom before Tanya came upstairs. Lying back in bed, with the lights off, he played back what had just happened, in his mind. He felt a bit guilty, like he'd crossed a line. But he hadn't cheated, it was no different to looking at a magazine, or a porno mag, he told himself...

Tanya slipped into bed beside Matt. Oh good, he was asleep. He was snoring, which usually drove her crazy, but tonight she left him to it. As long as he was snoring, he was asleep, and she was feeling horny again. Sex between them had become so rare these last few months, and when they did try it seemed like they both made too much effort, making it awkward.

So much easier to just give herself a quick orgasm before she fell asleep. She slipped up the bottom of her short night slip and let her hand skim over herself.

Immediately her body responded, the familiar tug in the pit of her stomach before the rush of heat between her legs.

Slowly her fingers teased her swelling labia, parting them and slipping inside to ease out her wetness, spreading it over her clit...

NOW - TOUCH ME WHERE I TELL YOU

Tanya turned around when Mandy came into the staff kitchenette. 'How's the evening job going, Tanya?'

She looked around, embarrassed, not wanting anyone to hear. 'Shh, Mandy, someone will hear us! But it's going fine thanks, better than I thought!

Mandy laughed. 'You're a natural, I always thought so! And don't worry, no-one would ever guess in a million years. Would you ever have thought that's what I did in the evenings?

'No,' admitted Tanya, 'But I'm still terrified of being found out. The money's good, I must admit. It's helping pay for my flat, at least while I'm there.'

'Aw, are you still hoping to get back with him? Just don't ever think you'll meet someone else on the site, although Ibiza did you know! They don't encourage it of course, say it's dangerous, which it is if you think about it. That's why we don't tell them anything personal. You're being careful right?'

Tanya hesitated. 'Well, yes, I am, but there's this one guy... He's really nice, different to the usual ones. He really chats, you know? Asks me about my day, tells me about his. He was quite shy to begin with, didn't request anything for the first few weeks.'

'Careful, Tan, you sound like you're falling for him! You didn't tell him anything did you?'

'Oh no, I said I worked in a restaurant and bar. I'm being careful, don't worry. And thanks, Mands, I'm grateful, and enjoying it too, can you believe it!'

Tanya felt quite weird about what had happened with Action Man on his last visit. She'd really let herself go. She'd set quite strict rules as she hadn't wanted to attract the kind of guys who wanted her to do things she wasn't comfortable with. But she'd forgotten all about the rules when he'd made his first request...

Matt was having a beer with Sam at the local pub. As usual Sam had badgered him about never seeing him these days. 'I'm worried about you mate. Since you and Tanya separated you've spent too much time on your own.'

'I know, I'm just trying to get my head together. It's weird, you know, being on my own after so long with Tanya? I don't know if I'll get her back, or if I even want to now...

Sam frowned at him. 'Now why wouldn't you want Tanya back? She's hot, mate! You need to make an effort. Meet her for a drink or something. The longer you leave it the more chance there is of one of you meeting someone else. Then you'll never get back together.'

Matt looked down into his beer guiltily. 'The thing is, I have kind of met someone else... you know that website you told me about?'

Sam laughed incredulously. 'You've got to be kidding! You don't meet girls on a sex site, mate! Bloody hell, you need help! Who is she then? Give us a look!'

But Matt closed up, saying he didn't mean it really. There was no way he was going to let Sam see Savanna. He didn't actually want any blokes looking at Savanna. He wanted to take her away from the site. He was falling for her, if he was honest...

Tanya checked her webcams and smoothed her platinum wig, crossing her legs as she reclined on the couch. Would he visit tonight? She let her mind wander as she waited for viewers to come online.

It was true, what she'd said to Mandy, Action Man *was* different to the other guys. He really talked to her. She thought back to Matt, they used to talk to each other all the time, but it had stopped at some point. That's when things had started to go wrong...

They used to tell each other about their day when they got home from work. They used to drink wine, enjoy meals at the table, have fun together. And they used to fancy each other! When did that stop? Matt was a good-looking bloke, very good-looking truth be told...

'I haven't been able to stop thinking about you...'

He was online! She hadn't noticed, she'd been too busy thinking about Matt... 'Me too...' She smiled up at the camera, giving him a little wave.

Matt grinned, drinking in the sight of Savanna, looking cute and sexy. He loved her outfit tonight, what was it, some kind of tight mini dress with over the knee socks? God, he was hard just from looking at her for one second.

They chatted for a few minutes, catching each other up on their day - Action Man talking openly about his work, Savanna making up a few white lies about her job at the restaurant.

It was amazing, he made shipping sound really interesting. A thought occurred to her. Matt worked in shipping! How strange, talk about a coincidence! Come to think about it, Matt used to tell her about it and had made it sound quite interesting too. What if they knew each other? No way, impossible, that sort of coincidence only happened in the movies.

Action Man was flirting with her gently, telling her how cute she looked. She thanked him, smiling and saying she was a little tired, maybe she'd lie on the bed for a while. Did he mind?

Did he mind? Definitely not! 'Go ahead, Savanna, get yourself comfortable, the view just gets better!'

She laid back on the bed, propped up by the mass of cushions behind her. She was wearing a tight mini dress in baby pink tonight. She'd felt like going for the cute look after her ultra-sexy image the other night.

Her over the knee socks stopped mid-thigh, showing bare flesh to the bottom of her dress. She was wearing the heeled mary janes again and underneath she'd got a surprise for Action Man. If he made a private request that is...

Her viewer numbers increased suddenly and she received another couple of messages. She had to keep her other viewers happy so she spent a few minutes chatting and flirting gently. Luckily, because she had quite a few rules, she didn't attract the worst pervs, most of hers were quite tame.

Matt watched jealously as Savanna typed and smiled up at the camera, giving a little wave here and there. Who were these other bastards? Why didn't they go and view someone else? There were plenty of girls on the site. Savanna was his!

Listen to yourself, you're losing it. She's not yours, you idiot, she gets paid by all these guys, just like you pay her. The voice of reason spoke sternly to him but still, he felt irritated and sighed with relief when his tablet pinged again.

'Busy night tonight, sorry!' She gave him a little rueful pout and wriggled around on the bed to give him a nice view of her thighs as her dress rode up. Him and all the other guys ogling her. There was that voice again.

Private request her. Private request her now! What could he ask her to do? He still felt uncomfortable about asking her to do things, even though that was the idea. The other night had been amazing. To think she'd done all that just for him. More than that, she'd broken her rules for him! It still made him hot to think about it and he'd enjoyed a very pleasurable replay in bed last night, as he'd lain there thinking about her.

Matt clicked on *private request* and typed quickly, looking up to see her reaction when she read his message.

Her heart lurched when she read it. He was so sexy, so different. No-one else had ever asked her for this. This was more like a lover's request... To want her to touch herself where he told her, as they chatted, as if it were his hands on her body...

She nodded at the camera, smiling invitingly, and clicked over to *private view*. Reading his first message she traced her hand down, over her body, to the bottom of her dress.

Matt watched, entranced, as her hand did his bidding, slowly raising her dress up to reveal... Oh, fuck me! She was wearing crotch less panties! The slit in the panties revealed her dark bush as it escaped the lace slightly.

His cock was poking up through his shorts, rock solid and aching and he held it, trying to calm himself down. Not too fast, not too fast...

He started telling her what he was doing as well. 'I'm holding my cock, it's so bloody hard. Lift your dress up further, I want to see more of your beautiful body.'

She was turning him on big time! This was so sexy! She slowly teased her dress up, until it reached to just below her breasts, looking up at the camera enquiringly. She felt totally aroused already, knowing he could see her bush where her panties parted. Her nipples were hard as she imagined him seeing them when she lifted her dress higher. She checked her screen.

Easing herself up, she lifted her dress up and over her hair, so that she was wearing only her underwear and socks and shoes. She leaned back on the cushions, feeling hot and a familiar wetness gathering between her legs, as she followed his next instruction.

Oh God, he groaned out loud. The sight of her nipples pushing through the slits in the front of her bra was a massive turn on. His cock was already leaking cum and he pushed his shorts down, gripping it firmly.

'I want to touch your nipples, touch you through the slit in your panties...' He gripped his cock as he watched her start to touch her nipples.

She smiled lazily up at him as she stroked them, making them stand out pink and firm through the slits. He gasped, moving his hand faster.

Her hand wandered down tantalisingly to her panties as she bent her knees up, parting her legs to give him a view of her glistening bush through the slit in her panties. She wanted him to see it, wanted him to see how turned on she was by him, her faceless stranger.

He was going to come. 'I'm going to come! You're too hot, Savanna!' He squeezed the tip of his cock, leaning back as his cum started to spurt, gasping as he gave himself over to his orgasm.

He was coming! Over her! She felt so hot and sexy! She touched herself, feeling her wetness, knowing he was coming right now. She plunged her fingers inside her, groaning as she came immediately, thrusting herself up towards the camera.

Matt watched her creamy cum ooze out over her fingers as she orgasmed and shuddered as she finished. He wanted to fuck her! Shit, he wanted to fuck her really badly...

SAM

Sam was intrigued, he had to admit it. He'd only sent Matt the website link for a laugh, thinking it kind of cool that his sister's mate worked on it.

But now he was wondering two things... Who was his sister's mate and who was the chick that Matt had got the hots for?

After his drinks at the pub with Matt, he arrived home and decided to have another look at the site. He typed in the web address for *Watch Me Want Me* and watched as the page loaded with photos of all the hot girls.

Yeah well, he had to admit, it was pretty tempting to look at them. There were girls to suit every taste, and he scrolled slowly, appraising them as he went...

Hmm... Peaches... cute, but a bit too *baby doll* for his liking... Alexa was hot, he paused, taking in her slim, toned body, barely covered in some kind of mesh dress, hair falling over her shoulders. He peered at the screen more closely, bloody hell, he could see everything through that dress! Nipples, hair, the lot!

His cock was paying attention too, he noticed, feeling it pressing uncomfortably against his jeans zipper. Down, boy! We're not here for that.

Star, mmm, nice... totally see-through dress... massive nipples sticking right out, this one was not shy... maybe it was her that Matt fancied...

He paused over the platinum blonde, Savanna... no doubt about it, totally hot, tiny silver top over miniscule hot pants... but platinum blondes had never been his thing and he carried on scrolling.

Nadia... he stopped, now this was a chick he could go for. Masses of tumbling red hair, thick dark lashes, shiny red lips, just his thing. He liked a bit of make-up on a girl, lots actually, if he was honest. He wasn't one for the natural look, found it a turn on when a chick tarted herself up.

He gave it a moment's thought, and then, partly because he was slightly beered up after his night out with Matt, decided to register with the site. Coming up with a name was easy, Fireman, and no-one else had taken it, so Fireman he was.

Okay, he'd put up some credit, just so he could check out how the whole *live* thing worked. It's just for research, he told himself, concern for a mate, nothing more.

He stared at the screen, watching Nadia in action. She was slowly gyrating to music which only she could hear, swinging her hair over her face and lifting her dress up teasingly every now and then to give her viewers a glimpse of her lace clad buttocks.

He was tempted to send her a message but, erring on the side of caution watched silently for a few minutes before signing out and hitting the sack.

THEN - ENDINGS AND BEGINNINGS

It was no surprise, if they were both honest, when they made the decision to separate. They'd finally sat down and talked honestly about how miserable they both were. How they felt they'd drifted apart, didn't seem to have anything to talk about anymore. Tanya had cried openly and Matt had cried privately. They still loved each other, they both admitted, but was that enough?

They left a lot unsaid, drew conclusions that could have been wrong.

Tanya was sure that Matt didn't fancy her anymore. Matt was sure that Tanya wasn't interested in him anymore.

They agreed to a separation period of about three months, to give themselves some space. Both agreeing that it would do them good, they'd probably miss each other so much they'd be back together before then.

'I'll move out,' Tanya informed Matt, through red-rimmed eyes. 'A friend of mine is going overseas for work for a year, I'm sure I can rent her flat from her.'

The first night in her friend's flat was so miserable and lonely, Tanya felt desperate. She wanted to phone Matt, tell him she missed him, they'd made a mistake. But she knew that they needed time apart, she just had to be strong.

It felt really odd, sad too, walking indoors on the first night after Tanya had left. The house felt completely silent, empty, almost unlived in. He walked around, picking things up, little curios they'd picked up on their holidays. Remembering happier times made him feel so bloody sad, he was tempted to call her, tell her he missed her.

It was a couple of weeks later, during the lunch hour, while Tanya was eating her sandwich in the staff kitchenette, that Mandy made the crazy suggestion. Tanya nearly choked on her mouthful of sandwich as she looked at Mandy in horror.

'Are you mad? Me? Work on a sex site? Why on earth would you think I'd ever do that, Mandy?'

Mandy grinned, sitting down beside her. 'Calm down, babes, it's not as crazy as it sounds. I do it.'

'Don't lie!' Tanya laughed, 'There's no way you work on a sex site. Those girls are all immigrants, sex-trafficked or something, or else they're hookers!'

Mandy shushed her, someone was coming. 'Meet me after work for a drink, we'll have a chat. Even if you don't think you want to do it, let me tell you about it at least, then you can decide. And let's have a drink anyway, stop you going home to spend the evening alone every night.'

Tanya agreed to the drink, agreeing that some company would be good. Since she and Matt had separated, she'd spent every evening on her own in her friend's flat. She'd mentioned to Mandy that funds were a little tight, not thinking for one minute that Mandy would suggest such an extreme way of earning a few extra quid!

Matt hadn't visited *Watch Me Want Me* once since Tanya had gone. He couldn't explain it, he just hadn't felt like it. But as time had gone along, he'd found himself thinking about the girls he'd looked at on the site...

He was a healthy male, he had needs, but he never once considered the idea of going out and chatting up a chick somewhere. Funny, he and Tanya hadn't actually discussed that part of the separation at all. Were they being faithful to each other while they were apart? Was Tanya? What if she met someone else?

He felt a niggling jealousy at the thought of Tanya being with another bloke. Shit! It had never occurred to him that she might be going out with her mates for drinks. She was pretty good looking, gorgeous if he was honest. She'd have blokes hitting on her no problem.

Meanwhile he was sitting at home like a monk, not having any fun. Tanya was funny, sexy too, he'd fancied her the first time he'd met her. He should never have agreed to the separation. How long had it been, two weeks or so? Bloody hell, still over two months to go before they'd agreed to meet and talk.

Mandy brought the glasses of wine to the bar table and swung herself up onto the bar stool beside Tanya. 'So how's it going really, hun? You missing him?' She looked sympathetically at Tanya as she sipped her wine.

Tanya nodded into her wine glass. 'I am missing him, Mands, but I know we really need this time apart. We'd virtually stopped noticing each other, never talked, and never had sex anymore. Hopefully we'll both realise how much we miss each other and be able to start again.'

'But, Mands,' Tanya looked up at her friend. 'When I said funds were tight, I wasn't thinking of working in the sex trade!'

'Listen, do I look like a hooker to you?' Mandy smiled at her friend. 'The site I work on is pretty high class. I kind of get a kick out of it, you know? I get to dress up and spend the evening looking hot and drinking wine. All I have to do is look sexy, give my viewers a little glimpse of this and that and chat to them if they want. They're not all perverts, plus I earn pretty decent money!'

'But what if someone recognised you?' Tanya looked aghast at the thought. 'Doesn't that worry you?'

Mandy took out her tablet and typed quickly, bringing up a website. 'Look at this, tell me which one's me.' She handed the tablet to Tanya and picked up her wine, drinking, while she watched Tanya scroll through the photos.

'There's no way you're on here!' Tanya handed the tablet back to Mandy. 'Show me!'

Mandy scrolled quickly, clicking on an image and handing the tablet silently back to Tanya.

'You're Nadia? You can't be! There's no way that's you! She's got red hair! And she's a bloody sex goddess! Not that you're not, you know, oh, you know what I mean...' Tanya looked up at Mandy, wanting to believe her but not wanting to believe her.

'Honey, I'm wearing a wig! And tons of make-up! False lashes, you name it, it's so easy to change your appearance! That's half the fun of it, the thrill too. Each night I work I get to dress up in whatever I feel like, choose my persona, depending on my mood.'

'But what do you do? Show me!' Shit, Mandy looked super-hot as Nadia, she still couldn't believe it was really her. 'Show me one of the rooms.'

Mandy clicked on a name and they were in one of the girls' rooms. They both watched as *Star* moved to the bed in the centre of the room, reclining on it sexily as she smiled at the camera. Suddenly she waved at the camera. 'Hi, Nadia!' The message appeared on the right of the screen.

'She's talking to Nadia, she knows it's you?' Mandy nodded.

'We chat to our viewers, their names appear on our laptops so we know who's watching us. They don't all want to chat, some just watch for a few minutes, some for an hour or so. All of us girls can chat to each other too, that's how Star knew I was online. It helps when it's a quiet night, believe me, or when we want to share something funny, or weird maybe.'

Mandy's screen went black and a message came up *private request in progress.*

'What does that mean?' Tanya was intrigued and a little uncomfortable. Private request? What on earth was Star doing? And who was she doing it for?

'Ok, that means that one of Star's viewers has private requested her. He'll have asked her to do something just for him. He has to pay, of course. Depending on the request the amount varies. Star sets her own rules so she never does anything she's not comfortable with.'

The two women stared silently at the blank screen, each wondering what Star was doing.

Oh fuck it, why not have a look at the website again? Surely that was better than going down the pub and ending up chatting to real chicks. Whatever he and Tanya had agreed, he kind of knew that going out on the pull was not meant to be on the cards.

He didn't even feel like going out on the pull. He had no desire to interact with girls at the bar, chatting them up and going through the whole process. He just wanted a bit of sexual release...

Typing in the website name he settled himself at his desk with a beer, the familiar feeling of surreptitious excitement running through his body. What was the name of that hot chick he'd looked at last time? Star, that was it...

Star's long, dark, curls, fell in a shining mass around her bare shoulders. She was reclining on the bed, wearing some kind of sheer baby doll outfit. He had no idea what it was but it was certainly doing the trick, if his hard cock was anything to go by.

He watched her for a while, imagining what she was wearing underneath the sheer fabric. Was she naked? Was she wearing sexy underwear? As he watched, she rolled over onto her front and he caught a glimpse of her firm buttocks as her little dress rode up. His cock hardened some more and he pushed his shorts down to hold it.

Star turned over again and waved at the camera, smiling, then typed something, but it wasn't to him. Realising that she might be about to receive a private request from someone, Matt typed quickly.

He leaned back, ready for the show and Star didn't disappoint. Slowly she untied the satin ribbons running down the front of her sheer little dress...

'What d'you think she's doing?' Tanya whispered to Mandy, trying to imagine what might be going on. Then she thought about the man who'd made the private request. What would he be like? Some disgusting lecherous perv no doubt.

'She's probably undoing those cute little satin ribbons, for starters.' Mandy sounded very knowledgeable. 'Then, depending on what her viewer's asked for, she'll either be cavorting around in her underwear, or even taking it off slowly and teasingly.'

'You mean she's naked?' Tanya was shocked, but also a little excited at the thought. She had to admit it gave her a little frisson, a thrill... There was something about the idea of laying there looking so hot, knowing that someone found you desirable...

Bloody hell, Star didn't hold back! Matt gasped as he came, his sperm running over his fingers as he reached for a tissue. Her naked body glimmered under the electric lights. She had stripped completely for him and touched her body everywhere, her fingers probing inside herself, glinting wetness as she drew then back out.

Matt logged off. He'd got what he wanted, a release of his tension. Suddenly he just wanted to grab something to eat and to watch some TV. He fleetingly thought of Tanya, wondering what she was doing right now...

'Why don't you come with me tomorrow evening? See what it's like? You can watch me get ready, even watch me in action if you want, if it won't make you feel weird.' Mandy could sense that Tanya was intrigued, even a little interested.

Tanya gulped down her wine, emptying the glass. 'Savanna.' she said suddenly, looking at an advert for a South African cider, on the wall next to them. 'That's what I'll call myself, if I decide to do it. Savanna.'

THEN - REAL CAMERAS, IMAGINARY CAMERAS

Tanya felt a like a proper little prude when Mandy introduced her to a few of the girls the next evening. Of course, she wasn't Mandy, she was Nadia now, she must remember that. Mandy had said that they only used their *show names*, as they called them, so no-one knew their real names.

She'd smiled and said hi to some of the girls but they all looked so hot and sexy compared to her in her work clothes. Some were just wearing sexy underwear with stockings and heels, others were dressed in various costumes, one was a school girl, another a nurse.

Nadia appeared before Tanya's very eyes, as Mandy changed into her chosen outfit for the evening. She expertly applied her heavy make-up, added false lashes and then, finally, fitted on her wig of vibrant red hair.

Tanya gaped in astonishment, as well as a little envy. 'Oh my God! You look so amazing! Where do you get the outfits from? That dress is amazing, and those boots, I love them!'

Nadia grinned. 'I knew you'd like all this! Think of it as big girls playing dressing-up. We loved it as kids, now we get to do it all over again. Except this time, we get to look bloody sexy as hell! Some of the clothes we buy ourselves, as well as the wigs and all the underwear. But there's also a whole walk-in closet stacked with outfits and footwear. It's every girl's dream!'

'But where d'you buy the stuff from?' Tanya felt like such an innocent. Maybe she should've been buying stuff like this to wear for Matt, maybe he wouldn't have lost interest in her then. Maybe she'd have paid him more attention too, she admitted to herself, if she'd been walking around at home dressed like Nadia. She'd have been feeling so hot, he wouldn't have stood a chance.

'Oh, we get stuff online, there are hundreds of websites selling sexy stuff. Haven't you ever bought anything sexy for yourself and your man to enjoy? You must have!' Nadia's astonished look made Tanya feel even more of an innocent. She really needed to grow up a bit, sexy herself up a bit.

'Ok, I'm going into my room now. You can come in and see it but you won't be able to stay in there with me, my viewers might find that a bit weird. Or, come to think of it, some of them might like it, might private request us to do stuff together!'

Tanya flushed with embarrassment. Nadia (she had to get used to calling Mandy that when she was here, that is, *if she was going to do this*...) seemed so casual about it all, so comfortable with her sexuality. She wished she could be as confident. Maybe it was the outfit, and the wig, it was like becoming a different person if she thought about it. You could be anyone you wanted to be... the thought excited her.

She followed behind Nadia, admiring her all-lace dress which clung to her body, showing every small curve. Below the red of the lace, she could see her gold G-string but when Nadia turned round to talk to her, she was aware of how clearly she could see Nadia's nipples poking slightly through the holes in the lace.

'I'm using red lighting tonight,' Nadia explained, as she set up her room to her satisfaction, 'It'll look extra hot with my outfit, as well as give a little of the *red light district* feel to the whole experience for my viewers. Plus, I've got a bit of a thing going with a guy called Fireman, so it's kind of a little bit of fun for him too.'

Nadia flung herself down on the gold velvet chaise longue, stretching out her legs sexily. 'How do I look?' she asked Tanya, laughingly.

'You look fantastic!' Tanya replied, admiringly. She looked around the room with interest, noting the cameras, trying to imagine herself in a room like this with men watching her. 'So, who's Fireman? What d'you mean by *a thing*?'

Nadia laughed. 'Oh, he's just a fun guy, enjoys a bit of flirting, not been on the site for long.'

'Ok, babes, time to go! Help yourself to a glass of wine in the dressing room if you want. I know! Why not try on a few outfits, see how it feels, while you're here? I've arranged for Dax, our boss, to have a quick chat with you as well. Don't worry, he's already said you're perfect, he checked you out when you came in with me!'

Don't worry? Her legs felt weak at the thought of talking to a man who had said she was perfect to work on his sex site. But her interest propelled her into the dressing room, as directed by Nadia, and she poured herself some wine to calm her nerves.

'Hi, darling, I hear you're joining us in our quest to bring happiness to all the guys out there! Tanya, isn't it?' Dax swooped on her, holding her shoulders and kissing her on the cheek. He wasn't what she was expecting at all. She'd pictured a swarthy, tough looking Eastern European, instead he was an extremely handsome Londoner, young, thirties at a guess.

Tanya smiled, liking him even in her nervousness. 'Hi, Dax, yes, it appears so! But I don't know if I'll be any good at it, I've never done anything like this before.' She looked up at him worriedly, but he put her mind at rest.

'Don't worry, none of the girls here had done this before they started. You'll learn as you go, find out what works for you and your viewers. You'll be a natural, I can tell, you're going to be very popular.'

After a little chat, Dax left Tanya to her wine and the wonders of the dressing room, telling her to have fun. 'Try on a few outfits, see what styles suit you.

You'll have to get yourself anything else you need online, I'm sure Nadia told you.'

There was no-one around so she quickly stripped off her clothes, including her bra, feeling a mounting excitement as she slipped the sheer dress over her head. It was so tight that she had to smooth it down firmly to cover herself. She stepped into the pair of heels she'd put ready and stood back to admire her reflection.

Her breasts were sexily pushing against the sheer white fabric, her nipples clearly visible and immediately hard. She almost gasped out loud, surprised at how sexy she looked. The panties spoiled the look and, with a quick glance around to make sure she was still alone, she slipped them down her legs and stepped out of them.

Her physical reaction to her reflection in the mirror was instant, a little jolt in her stomach, followed by a pull lower down in her vagina. She could see her pubic hairs clearly, she might as well be naked, but the dress made everything look so amazingly hot. Just imagining a guy looking at her like this made her feel sexy, a little slutty and totally aroused. The dress reached to just below her bush and she leaned back slightly, parting her legs a little, so that it rose up just enough to give a glimpse of her hair covered mound.

Tentatively she touched herself between her legs, knowing that she was already wet. No, stop, Tanya, you can't do it here. Or could she? She looked around, making sure there was no-one around, and glancing up to make sure there were no cameras in the dressing room.

She touched herself again, surprised at the fire that shot through her. She looked like a sex goddess, couldn't believe how it made her feel to look so hot. What if she had guys watching her right now? Could she do it? Should she do it? She tested the feel of her fingers slipping down to touch herself as she watched herself in the mirror. It was a massive turn-on and she let her fingers probe her lips and slip inside, feeling excitement run through her body. She leaned back against the packed clothes rail, parting her legs still further, as she quickly brought herself to orgasm.

Anxious that someone might come in, she removed her hand from her still throbbing vagina and pulled her panties back on, suddenly wanting to get her own clothes on again. Once she was dressed, she made a note of some online stores from the list on the wall, scribbled a note for Nadia, and left for her flat.

She was feeling hyped when she got home, but made herself shower and get something to eat before finally pouring a glass of wine and sitting at her laptop. She clicked away, bringing up page after page of gorgeous outfits, lingerie, sexy thigh high boots and wigs.

Oh, but the wigs... how could she decide what would suit her? Did she want to look like Cher? Tempting, but then, the long, raven curls of this wig were gorgeous... But then again, oh yes, here it was, it was perfect. The sleek, peroxide

33

blonde wig could be worn swept to the side, or with a fringe, and its longer bob length was just right. She clicked on *buy* and added it her basket.

Stop, Tanya, enough! She checked her basket to see just how much she had spent and decided it was time to stop shopping. Arranging for her parcel to be delivered to her at work, she logged off, it was getting late and she wanted to relax for a while with her wine, thinking over her strange day.

Matt took his time scrolling through this time, looking at the photos of the different girls on the site. He silently admitted to himself that he felt like a bit of a perv, choosing a girl to wank off to. But hey, they chose to be on the site, right? They knew the guys who watched them weren't looking for friendship.

He paused over the photo of a girl called Nadia. Nice red hair, very hot. She was *live* and he clicked through to see what she was doing in her room. Wow, nice red dress, all see through lace with tits nicely visible. She was reclining on a chaise longue, drinking wine and typing on her laptop. Chatting with one of her viewers of course, Matt knew how it worked now. Her screen went dark and he lost interest. Someone else was getting a nice private show, he'd look elsewhere.

Tanya had nearly finished the bottle of wine and was feeling nicely drunk. She was impatient to receive the items she'd ordered and decided to have a practice run with what she had to hand. The short little sundress was a favourite from last summer - cute but sexy. She undressed completely and slipped it on, leaving most of its buttons unfastened at the top and bottom. She found one of her lacy thongs, not worn for a long time now, she sadly acknowledged, and wandered back through to the lounge.

Sitting back on the couch, she imagined that a camera was *live*, facing her, with unknown men watching her. She took a mouthful of wine and placed her glass down on the coffee table. Playing with the top of her dress, she encouraged it to fall open so that her breasts were exposed. Tracing her fingers over them, she felt her nipples respond immediately, and opened her legs so that the dress fell apart, uncovering her lace covered pussy.

Angel was anything but angelic, Matt decided, having clicked on her cute photo and been presented with a blonde babe playing with her selection of dildos and vibrators. He felt his cock turn hard as she placed one over her panties, between her legs. Slowly she teased herself, smiling at the camera, before slowly unfastening her blouse to reveal two large breasts encased in a see-through bra.

Matt held his breath as Angel shrugged off her blouse. She kept her tiny skirt on and continued to play with the vibrator. His laptop pinged and he read the message she'd sent him. 'Want to play Action Man?' He froze for a moment, it was always weird, as if they could see you.

'I'll play, Angel,' he typed, before clicking on *private request* and asking for something which she was obviously dying to do anyway.

34

Through half-closed eyes, Tanya lowered her hand, placing it between her legs, keeping her other hand on her beasts. She touched herself through her lace thong, feeling her body respond. Is this what I'll do for real, she wondered? Am I brave enough? Probably not, her mind answered, but by now she was feeling hot and horny...

Matt gawped at the screen, Angel was leaving nothing to the imagination as she teased and probed herself with the vibrator. He could see the damp seeping through the gusset of her panties, and his cock ached as he grasped it. Moving his hand faster, he watched, mesmerised, as she pulled her panties to one side and slowly inserted the vibrator inside herself.

She was close to coming now, couldn't stop herself, the combination of the wine, her outfit and the pretence of the camera were too much. Moaning softly, as the first spasm ran through her body, she impatiently pulled her panties to one side and slipped two fingers into her vagina. Arching her back she came in waves, gasping, and opened her eyes to stare straight into the imaginary camera.

Honey McGregor

NADIA

It was true, what she'd said to Tanya about the guy calling himself Fireman. He was just a fun guy, and it was kind of nice to have someone who didn't just say sex stuff the whole time.

He'd only appeared on the site recently and seemed to have a bit of a thing for her. She'd checked with the other girls and none of them recalled him paying them any attention in particular.

He certainly added a bit of a frisson to her evenings working for the site and she was aware that she looked forward to his chats now. Of course, she knew he could be anyone, or anything, man, woman, old or young, who knew?

She'd been doing it long enough to know that you didn't get involved with the guys online. You didn't trust a word they said and you never told them anything personal. She only hoped that Tanya would take all her advice on board.

Her laptop pinged and she grinned. Talk of the devil! 'Hi, Fireman, can't keep away can you?'

Sam grinned, at home, he loved the way this chick played. He typed back his response, knowing she'd have a comeback. Funny really, it was hardly sexual between them, more like banter. Maybe that's how it had started for Matt...

Nadia finished her shift on a high. It had been fun again, this guy was cool. Shame really, they'd probably get on really well in real life...

Honey McGregor

NOW - MEET THE NEW GIRL

'Parcel for you in reception, Tanya,' the receptionist rang off and Tanya looked around guiltily before getting up and heading for the stairs. Damn, the whole afternoon to get through still, before she could go home and open up her package.

Finally, the working day was over and she headed straight to her flat, impatient to try on her purchases. Standing back, her gaze wandered over the assortment of items laid out on the bed. She'd bought herself a couple of dresses in lycra, one black and one baby pink, plus a gorgeous pair of black thigh high boots and some clear perspex pole dancing heels.

Her lingerie selection was quite random, one set being of sheer white fabric, clingy and totally see-through, while one of the others was the full push-up bra with matching thong, in creamy coffee coloured satin with black lace trim. One thing was for sure, it was all hotter than any underwear she'd ever owned before and she couldn't wait to wear it.

She picked up the black hot pants she'd added to the basket at the last minute, and laid them out with the silver halter top she'd chosen to accompany them. Perfect, it was *all* perfect! But most perfect of all was the wig, in all its peroxide blonde absolute perfection.

Impatient now, she showered quickly, before trying on the black lycra dress and the boots. They fitted like a second skin and she admired her reflection in the full-length mirror. Now she picked up the wig, carefully placing it over her hair and tucking the escaping strands of her own hair out of sight.

She stood back and looked at her reflection in the mirror. 'Hello, Savanna,' she whispered to the stranger staring back at her.

Oh God, suddenly she felt terrified. Could she really do this? Was she actually going to be able to sit around in a room while blokes watched her on their computers? Mandy did, she reminded herself, and seemed to enjoy it too.

Okay, they won't know who I am, no-one will recognise me. Bloody hell, I don't even recognise myself! You can do it, Tanya. She lifted her head and looked at herself again. You can do this, Savanna.

Matt decided to take Sam up on his plea for a drink or two after work. He hadn't been out with the lads for a week or so and they were hassling him. It's not like he had anything else to do anyway, well, apart from his new little online hobby.

Good beer, good mates and a good laugh worked their magic, as they always did, and Matt returned home to the empty house feeling nicely inebriated. He watched TV as he ate the burger he'd picked up on the way home, and crawled into bed. Maybe he'd just have a quick look online...

His thoughts strayed to Tanya, as they still often did. Was she okay? Was she missing him? Maybe he should text her, but no, they'd agreed to give each other space, time to work out how they felt about their relationship. He should give it time, try and ignore the empty place in the bed beside him.

What would she think about him going online and watching chicks on a sex site? She'd be horrified, disgusted with him, would probably never want to talk to him again. He must never tell her. He just had needs, that was all, if they got back together again, he'd stop.

And so tonight was the night. This was it. Mandy was really sweet, helping her to get ready, exclaiming over the wig she'd bought, loving her outfits and telling her she looked amazing. Best of all, she told Tanya that she would never have known it was her, if she didn't know already.

Reassured, Tanya entered her room, again, assisted by Mandy who helped her check her cameras. They'd set her *rules* the previous evening, so that hopefully no-one would make any private requests that she was uncomfortable with. She was definitely one of the tamer options for the viewers, not really offering anything other than looking sexy and teasing.

Okay, I'm Savanna now. Tanya's gone for the evening. Taking a deep breath, she took a last look around her room and clicked *live*. The cameras winked into life and her laptop brought up a small window that showed what her viewers could see.

That is if she ever got any viewers... It had been over an hour and not one person had even stopped by for a quick look. Still, it was early days, and in the meantime it was quite nice to just sit and enjoy her wine and magazine.

Hello there, I haven't seen *you* before. Matt's eyes skimmed over the photo of Savanna, liking what he saw. Bloody hell, she was perfect, gorgeous, and those hot pants, fuck! Thigh high boots and a silver top showing a hint of erect nipple, he could go for this... But it was the hair... peroxide blonde, it was his biggest fantasy... *she* was his biggest fantasy, and she was right there, just for him, all he had to do was click the photo...

Excitedly he clicked on the photo, to be taken to Savanna in her room. He drew in a breath, she was even more gorgeous to watch live.

Oh God, oh God, someone was online watching her. She froze, her glass halfway to her lips, suddenly unsure of what to do. Her hand was trembling as she tried to take a sip from her wine glass and she glanced at the camera, trying to look casual.

Matt smiled as he saw her register that she had a viewer. She looked like a rabbit caught in the headlights, she looked so nervous. Maybe it was her first night? She had such a beautiful face he thought, as she looked up at the camera, trying to smile.

40

Savanna didn't know what to do. Should she chat to him? Try to keep him online? Mandy hadn't been too clear about that part, had just said she should just do what she felt comfortable with. Right now the only comfortable thing would be to switch off the camera and run!

Matt could almost read her thoughts, he felt, as he watched her eyes register panic. Suddenly he just wanted to put her at her ease. Forget the sex for a minute, Matt, talk to the poor girl. He typed a message.

She read his message and smiled, feeling calmer. 'Hi, Savanna, is this your first night? I haven't seen you before? I'm quite new to this too!'

He sounded sweet. 'Hi, Action Man, yes, you guessed it! My first night and I'm terrified, I don't know what I'm doing!' She took another gulp of wine and tried to breathe. That was probably all wrong, he'd lose interest, want someone more sophisticated.

But his message came back, 'You're doing fine! Don't be nervous! What are you reading?'

Relief flooded through her, he was nice! He wasn't even talking dirty! 'Marie Claire, just wanted something to help me feel relaxed!'

Marie Claire? Tanya always used to read that. Funny how she still popped into his head all the time. 'Well, I hope it helps! You look gorgeous by the way, but I'm sure all the guys tell you that!'

All the guys? 'You're my first viewer so no-one's ever told me that! Thank you, you're sweet!' She smiled up at the camera and gave him a little wave. She settled back on her couch and crossed her legs, unknowingly giving Matt a flash of her panties.

Matt felt a twinge of desire as he glimpsed her panties. Fuck, she didn't even know how sexy she was! Her black dress hugged her body in all the right places and just the sight of her thighs, bare above *those* boots, was enough to get him painfully hard.

But something made Matt hold back tonight, there was something vulnerable about Savanna and he didn't want to spoil it all by just getting off on her. Feeling all decent and noble he carried on chatting to her, enjoying their rapport

She was really enjoying herself, she realised, as his last message made her laugh out loud. No way would she have ever thought that her first night might turn out to be just having a nice chat with a really funny guy.

But her heart sank when her laptop screen showed that she had three other viewers... Now what? She couldn't just stay on the couch, chatting away to Action Man on her laptop, could she? She typed a quick message to him, 'We have company, I'll have to act interesting for a while!'

Jealousy. Immediate, hot, jealousy. Why couldn't these blokes look at someone else? It wasn't as if there was a shortage of girls on the site. Couldn't he have had her to himself, at least for her first night? 'Don't worry, I'm here. Don't give them anything too interesting to look at, they might stay!'

She giggled, he really was sweet. But he was kind of missing the point here... she was supposed to give her viewers something to look at... Self-consciously she stood up, picked up her magazine and laptop and placed them on the bed before sitting down beside them.

Then, slowly, she laid down on her front to leaf threw the magazine, bending her legs up behind her. She hoped she wasn't showing too much, should have practiced some of these moves beforehand, she realised.

Matt was holding his breath as she moved to the bed and laid down. Her tight dress had ridden up to partly expose her buttocks and she looked too fucking sexy for words. He wanted to reach out and touch her bare skin where it appeared above her boots. Wanted to run his fingers up those bare thighs, caress those firm buttocks, slip his fingers down between them...

He groaned, his cock was throbbing with desire. Fuck! Normally he'd just take his pleasure right now, if it was anyone else... But he couldn't bring himself to do it, didn't think he could carry on chatting with her if he'd just wanked off to her. He stared at the screen with jealous intensity...

Her laptop was now showing that she had ten viewers, maybe she should stop checking, it just made her more nervous. Not sure what to do next, she rolled onto her back and lifted her magazine up as if she was reading it in the air.

Oh God. No. Did she even realise what she was doing? Every move she made seemed laced with sexual teasing, seemed designed to turn her viewers on even more. He couldn't stand it. But what could he do? There was a star button to click to show appreciation and he clicked it, wanting to show her how much he liked her.

Hearing a series of gentle pings from her screen, she checked it and was surprised to see that she'd been starred five times. She knew what it meant, that guys watching her liked her. She guiltily admitted to herself that it felt pretty good. She felt sexy, desirable and, dare she admit it, a little hot. She clicked the star button to see who they were.

The names meant nothing to her, but then, another ping and another star, it was him! She smiled, turning around to the camera and giving another little wave, just for him. The message box appeared and she read the message expectantly.

'You're totally fucking hot, Savanna, I want to slip my hard cock right between those thighs and into your sweet cunt.'

Something was wrong, she was sitting up and her face was flushed. Matt felt frustration course through him as he watched helplessly. Some bastard had said something to her, he was sure. Something bloody disgusting no doubt. She looked like she was about to cry...

Horny Man, not Action Man. She'd assumed it was from him, hadn't even checked the name, felt so relieved that he hadn't sent the message. She sat up in shock and embarrassment, not sure what to do, feeling her face flush hotly as tears rushed to her eyes. Pull yourself together Savanna, you can handle this, you're just playing a game remember?

She smiled up at the camera and typed a reply. 'Hi, Horny Man, you know you can't do that...'

She was replying to the guy, what was she saying? He typed quickly, 'Are you okay?'

'I'm fine, just one of the viewers getting carried away, I guess I need to toughen up a little, that's all!'

Tiredness swamped over her, the effects of the shock, the wine, her nervousness, everything really. Maybe she should call it a night, there was no hard and fast rule about how many hours they should work, it all depended on how much they wanted to earn, that was all.

Quickly she typed him another message. 'I'm going to go home now, enough for me for tonight I think, I hope you visit again! Thanks for being so nice to me! Night, Action Man x.'

'Night, Savanna, I'll be back soon! Sleep well! x.' He was disappointed, but a protective instinct made him feel pleased that no other bastards would be ogling her tonight.

Home. She fell onto her bed feeling totally shattered. Thoughts of Action Man swirled around in her brain, his sweetness, how he'd made her laugh. Had he found her hot? He'd said she looked gorgeous... She was still wearing her outfit, had just thrown her long summer coat over it to get home, stopping only to remove the wig, before leaving.

Matt got into bed and laid there wide awake, thinking of Savanna. He couldn't get her out of his mind, there was something so sweet and vulnerable about her. Plus the obvious, of course, she was totally fucking hot...

He brought up the photo of her, in her hot pants and silver top, on his tablet and gazed at it. Images of her in the black dress came into his mind, of the boots and her bare thighs, her buttocks peeking below her dress when she laid on the bed...

Sleepily she realised that her dress had ridden up a little so that her panties were showing and she tried to picture how she must have looked to him as he watched her. Maybe she should have shown him a little more, laid like this, showing him a glimpse of her lace panties.

The thought excited her and she opened her legs so that the dress rode higher. Dropping her hand, she touched herself through the lace, feeling suddenly horny. She imagined him watching as, slowly, she traced her fingers over her budding labia.

43

He couldn't help it, he was only human after all. He propped his tablet up against the pillow beside him and held himself. He drank in the sight of her jutting nipples as they pointed through the thin silver fabric. Grasping his cock he began to masturbate, picturing those bare thighs leading to the lace panties imagining her slowly peeling them down to reveal her sweet pussy, just for him... Her eyes seemed to smile into his as, a few moments later, he gasped and shot his creamy cum out over his hand. He woke in the night to find her still smiling at him...

She was swollen and throbbing with arousal as she pulled her panties aside and rubbed her fingers over herself. Imagining him watching her, she slipped her fingers in and out to spread her wetness, tracing small circles on her clitoris until suddenly her pelvis pushed upwards and her orgasm crashed over her Tiredness carried her off to sleep, her hand still on herself, as her mind drifted with thoughts of her faceless mystery man...

NOW - FRENCH MAID SEX

She was excited, could hardly stop the feeling bubbling up inside her all day. They'd taken things to a new level last night when they'd chatted. They'd both admitted that they had real feelings for each other. And she'd shown it with her actions as she'd granted his private request while he shared his feelings and what he was doing as he watched her...

She knew that he wanted them to meet up, but that was all very well for him, he knew what she looked like (well, what he *thought* she looked like), while she had no idea about him at all. To be honest, the more they chatted the more it seemed unimportant what he looked like or what age he was (although she sensed he was a similar age).

He'd asked her if he could buy her an outfit to wear just for him. They'd discussed how to go about it and had come up with a plan. The website *Privately Precious* offered the facility to purchase a gift card to be collected by the recipient, with the correct password.

He was going to choose the outfit tonight and give her the details, plus the password, so that she could buy it with the gift card. What would he choose? He'd loved everything she'd worn over the last couple of months so she had no idea what his perfect outfit of choice would be.

Matt browsed the site as soon as he got home, trying to make his final decision. He wanted something perfect for Savanna, that showed her how much he adored her, but that also showed how sexy she was.

He felt like a school boy preparing for his first date, trying to choose a gift for his girl. There were so many different sections, from costumes to lingerie sets, play sets, dresses, and little top and skirt sets. He'd love to buy the lot, have Savanna wear a different outfit for him every night for the rest of their lives.

He knew that Savanna wasn't his, and never would be, all the time she worked on *Watch Me Want Me*. She'd admitted last night that she had feelings for him, as he had for her. But she still wouldn't agree to meet him in person. He couldn't blame her, she didn't even know what he looked like.

A thought struck him, what if they met and she didn't fancy him? Every girl he'd ever been out with had met him first, then got to know him, Tanya included, of course. This was the other way round, but didn't it mean something, that they got on so well?

Another thought struck him, it was time for him and Tanya to talk. They were going to have to make contact, arrange to meet and talk about how they both felt after their time apart. Guiltily, he admitted to himself that the chances of them getting back together were slim now - now that he'd met Savanna...

He tried to picture Savanna in the black lacy bustier. It fitted the model tightly and pushed her breasts up so that her nipples peeped slightly above the lace trim. It was bloody sexy and had straps for suspenders, so he could get her some stockings too...

But it wasn't enough. Maybe he should choose something for her to wear over the top? He looked through the assortment of dresses, finding a kind of black satin gown, strapless, with a central wrap-over slit in its full skirt from knee to waist. He pictured it falling open as she sat on the couch or the bed...

The outfit was starting to come together, he thought excitedly, but what about panties? And shoes? Maybe he should choose those too. He looked at the footwear, pausing over the boots, but she already had a pair of hot, thigh high boots, no, something different...

The black suede stilettos were perfect, hot but not tarty. In fact, he realised, the whole outfit was classy, which was how he thought of Savanna. So, finally, the panties... he grinned to himself. If Sam could see him now, he'd think he'd lost it! He'd never hear the end of it if Sam knew he was buying a sexy outfit for a girl who worked on a sex site.

A daring thought struck him, making him instantly hard as he pictured it, and he made his decision about the panties, hoping that Savanna wouldn't be shocked by it...

What could she wear for him tonight? She no longer thought about her other viewers, in fact, Dax had taken her aside the other night before she left for home, saying she was dropping in popularity, asking if she was neglecting her viewers in favour of only certain ones. He hadn't exactly said he was unhappy, but...

It didn't matter, she knew she wasn't going to stay with Dax for much longer, she'd already made her mind up. She would decide what to do about Action Man and either arrange to meet or she would leave the site anyway. Okay, she corrected herself, she knew she *would* meet Action Man and then, whatever happened, she would never go back to Dax.

She opened up the cellophane wrapping on the costume she'd bought online last week. Maybe she should have a little fun with him tonight. She'd never really worn costumes, apart from the school girl look she'd tried out the one time. But this French maid's costume was really hot...

It was different now, Matt knew exactly what nights she was on and what time she'd be *live*, no wondering and guessing. He signed in at exactly seven o'clock and clicked straight on Savanna's photo. The sight that met him took his breath away.

Tanya was feeling happy and sexy as she set up her room and props for Action Man. She knew he'd be straight on at seven o'clock and she checked the time before picking up her feather duster and making a pretence of dusting.

Matt's heart swelled, along with his cock, as the live image appeared on his screen. She'd created this whole scene just for him. He watched her as she bent over to dust the small table, before stretching up to dust in the corner by the ceiling. The little skirt of her French maid's outfit rose to reveal her bare buttocks, as she stretched, and he groaned out loud.

'Savanna, you look hotter than ever, you're amazing!'

She smiled, thanking him and feeling happiness wash over her. She let him know that she'd only be live for two hours and, as was now their routine, Matt private requested her for the whole time.

They chatted a little, catching up on their respective days, and then she told him to sit back and enjoy the show.

The bodice of her dress was totally sheer, her nipples clearly visible, as she pretended to dust up above the camera. Matt's eyes were glued to his screen as her erect nipples teased him just out of reach. God, he wanted to touch them and lick them, to suck them until she groaned out loud...

Her breasts were perfectly lined up with the camera and she slowly lowered the bodice of her dress a little, releasing them to give him a perfect view. She felt daring and sexy as hell as she slowly traced her fingers over her nipples, enjoying the sensation as they hardened under her touch.

Matt gazed in longing at the screen, at the vision just out of his reach. His fingers grazed the screen, trying to imagining being able to touch her breasts, to suck her nipples into his mouth. Not long now and he would be able to, once they met... His cock was quivering with a life of its own as it rose up, begging to be released and touched. He watched her move away, and then, his interest quickening, observed her shifting the coffee table closer to where the camera must be.

Tanya stood up on the table, gauging the view for Action Man, hmm, not quite high enough for her plan, but still... She pulled her bodice down even lower, slowly revealing her bare stomach, and caressed her skin.

Damn, he wanted to see more, wanted her to be a little higher so that he could see what was happening lower down. His eyes followed her every move as her hands moved across her stomach, teasing the place where her dress gathered by pulling it down even lower, just out of his sight.

He was rock hard with arousal and stood up quickly, striping off his clothes so that he was naked. That was better, he was as close as he could be to her now. His cock stood up like a flag pole, begging for attention, and he held it, not wanting to rush things.

The camera beside the bed would be perfect for her plan, she realised, she just needed to move the other table a little. Pulling her dress back up for now, she bent over and shifted the table, knowing that she was giving Action Man a total view of her bare buttocks.

Matt groaned out loud as he drank in Savanna's smooth buttocks, framed by the tops of her lace hold-ups and the frothiness of her dress. He peered closer trying to see if she was wearing any underwear... God, he wanted to cup those beauties, spread them gently apart and slip his fingers between them...

She turned around so that she had her back to the camera beside the bed, and he was now looking at her hands, gently lifting the back of her dress to reveal the narrow band of lace where her G-string disappeared between her buttocks. 'Fuck me,' he whispered, touching his screen, 'I want you so badly.'

He wanted to tell her that he was naked, that she was turning him on badly. 'I'm so hard for you, baby, I want you badly...' Maybe he'd leave the naked bit out for now...

'I want you to want me,' her reply came back. 'Look what you're doing to me... I'm imagining this is your hand...'

She turned around so that she was facing the camera. This was it, this was what she'd planned to do for him tonight... She was wet with her own arousal as she lifted her dress...

He gasped, holding his cock so hard he had to tell himself to relax. He leaned forward, staring at the sight of Savanna's sweet pussy, covered in a small triangle of see-through white fabric. Her thighs were apart and her fingers stroked herself through her panties, her wetness glistening and soaking through it so that she might as well not be wearing any panties at all.

This was the closest she'd ever been to him, she realised, the closest view she'd ever shown him of herself. She was fully aroused, knowing that he was too, and, throwing all caution to the wind she began to masturbate freely, not caring how much she showed of herself.

Bloody hell, he could see everything through her soaked panties, and so closely! Her trimmed hairs covering her mound, her lips, as they swelled and parted, the swollen bud of her clitoris pushing through between them... His balls ached, his mouth was dry and his cock was dripping, as his hand slipped back and forth along its length.

'God, I love your body, I love your pussy, it's so fucking perfect, baby, I want to touch it so much. I'm naked and holding myself, imagining it's your hand holding me... I'm dripping for you...'

His words excited her even further as she rubbed her fingers over herself, spreading her silky creaminess all over the sheer gusset of her panties. Impatiently she pulled them aside, touching her naked sex for him.

Matt's cock was spilling out wildly as his hand moved faster, his eyes on Savanna's creamy, wet pussy so close to him on his screen. He watched her fingers stroking her clitoris more urgently and then drew a deep breath as her fingers slipped inside.

He couldn't stop himself from coming and released in repeated shudders, his eyes still glued to her fingers as they moved in and out of her beautiful pussy, her creamy cum running out over them as she, too, came.

She was panting and feeling overcome with weakness, her orgasm had been intense. He'd have seen everything so closely on his screen and she didn't even feel weird about it. They'd become so close, they could only become closer by actually being together in person. Soon...

Matt leaned back, breathing heavily, that had been amazing. They'd shared so much now, surely it was time to take things to the next level and meet in person... and soon...

Once they'd both cleaned up, they resumed chatting, sharing how good it had been for both of them and talking about meeting up. Soon, they both agreed, but first, Action Man gave her the details of the outfit he'd chosen for her.

Savanna thanked him and they arranged to meet online in two days, once she had received the outfit, so that she could wear it for him. Unspoken was the agreement that it would probably be the last time before they finally met face to face...

Honey McGregor

NOW - FINISHED

The outfit he'd chosen for her was gorgeous! She couldn't wait to wear it for him tonight. It was sexy but kind of classy, not cheap or tacky, it told her something about him, she'd known he was a decent bloke. She didn't know what had made him start using the website, but that was his business, after all, she'd been on it too, they each had their reasons.

But soon they wouldn't have a need for the website. She'd made her mind up that she was going to tell Dax she was leaving, just as soon as she'd made arrangements to meet up with Action Man.

Tonight was the night! Savanna would wear his outfit he'd chosen for her, they'd have one last wonderful night together online and then make their plans to be together in real life! He couldn't wait...

A more sobering thought was the knowledge that he needed to contact Tanya. They needed to talk and he knew that it was over, he'd moved on, she probably had too... He needed to get it over with and decided that sooner was better than later.

Tanya thought about Matt as she drank her coffee. She needed to tell him it was over. And she needed to do it today if possible. Her life had changed more than she could ever have imagined and she had changed along with it. She needed to be honest with him (within reason), and get things sorted between them.

His phone pinged and he read Tanya's message. It wasn't unfriendly but it was short and to the point. She suggested meeting at lunchtime to talk and he replied in agreement, pleased that they'd be able to get things over with before he met Savanna online tonight.

She was in meetings all morning and it was only as she headed out to meet Matt that she realised she had four missed calls from Mandy. She tried to call her back but Mandy's phone was busy. She'd catch up with her later, or tonight if Mandy was on too.

They met halfway between their places of work, The Colony Wine Bar being their old haunt, back in happier days when they used to meet regularly at lunchtime. Matt brought them drinks to their corner table and they both sat there wondering how to begin.

Tanya looked different, he thought, something had changed about her but he couldn't put his finger on it, it was like she was more... alive. She looked bloody good too, hot if he was honest, but he needed to tell her it was over before she said something and it got awkward.

He looked great, thought Tanya, watching him as he steered his way through the lunchtime crowd. He was being really nice, kind of gentle, oh hell, she needed to tell him quickly, before he said something awkward...

They both stared talking at the same time.

'Matt, there's something I need to...'

'Tans, I need to tell you something...'

They laughed, taking a mouthful of their drinks, before Tanya said, 'I'm so sorry, Matt, I have to tell you something.'

'Me too,' said Matt, and then, as realisation dawned, 'You've met someone else, haven't you?'

Tanya nodded, looking down into her glass. 'I'm so sorry, I didn't mean for it to happen. But he gets me, really gets me. I don't know where it's going but I have to find out.'

'It's okay,' Matt took her hand, 'I've actually met someone too, I didn't know how to tell you, I've been feeling bad about it. We just really get on well, she understands me so well, we talk for hours. I'm pleased for you, Tan, I really am, you deserve to be happy, we both do.'

'Oh, Matt, I'm pleased for you too!' She rubbed his arm affectionately, feeling relieved and genuinely happy for him.

Total relief flooded through both of them as they admitted that things hadn't been right between them for so long. That the separation had been the right thing to do, that they were happy for each other, that they were so pleased that they could part as friends and not enemies.

They parted with hugs and platonic kisses on the cheek, deciding that there was no rush for them to work out what to do about the house. Tanya could stay in her flat for now, as her friend was still overseas.

They both had attacks of the nerves after they went their separate ways, knowing they were now embarking on new chapters in their lives.

She missed another call from Mandy while she was in the shower, getting ready for her last evening on the site. What the hell was Mandy so anxious to get in touch with her about? She was running late, wanted time to get ready in her new beautiful outfit. She quickly texted Mandy, telling her she'd talk to her when she saw her later, if she was also on tonight.

Matt hummed happily to himself as he showered, thinking about the evening ahead. This was it, the culmination of everything he and Savanna had been sharing together over the last couple of months. One last night online, her in his chosen outfit, and then, finally, they would plan where to meet.

Tanya walked quickly towards the building that had so changed her life, impatient to get in and start preparing. She was carrying a large bag, with her new outfit and her wig safely inside, and hooked it over her arm when her phone rang. God, it was Mandy again, it must be important! Answering her phone, she turned the corner to head down the street and bumped into someone coming the other way.

'Tans, thank God!' Mandy looked frantic as she grabbed Tanya's arm, steering her around and walking them both quickly in the opposite direction.

Tanya tried to shrug her off. 'Mandy, what the hell's going on? What's the matter with you? I'm going to be late!'

But Mandy held her arm firmly and walked them both a few more steps before stopping and turning Tanya to face her, a panicked look on her face. 'Tanya, you can't go there, it's over, the police are all over the place!'

'What? No way, why? What's happening?' Tanya tried to concentrate on what Mandy was telling her.

The building had been raided by the cops. Mandy had been warned by one of the girls earlier today, hence her frantic attempts to contact Tanya all day. The site had been closed down, Dax had gone, the cops were crawling all over everything.

But Tanya was in a state of panic. She had to go in, had to get a message to Action Man! She tried to pull away from Mandy, tried to head back around the corner.

Mandy held her arm again, 'Tans, listen to me, you can't go in, don't you get it? The cops are there, the site's closed down, you can't get a message to anyone.'

Still holding her arm, Mandy gently walked her to the corner. 'Look!' Blue flashing lights and police vehicles were blocking the area outside the building. There were people milling around, some in uniform, people talking into radios.

As they watched they saw two of the girls being brought out of the building by police. Tanya slumped against Mandy, it was true!

'But, Mandy, I have to talk to him! We were going to make plans to meet up! What am I going to do?'

'I think we need a drink,' Mandy kept her arm on Tanya's, concerned that she still might try to head towards the building. They entered the first pub they came to, Mandy taking control and ordering them drinks, before finding them a table to sit at.

'Oh God, Mandy, I can't believe it!' Tanya's voice sounded strained to her own ears. Tears were welling up in her eyes as the reality of the situation sunk in. She was never going to meet Action Man, it was over before it had even started...

'Look,' Mandy tried to calm her down, 'For now, we need to be grateful that we weren't there when the cops came. We weren't doing anything illegal, as far as I know, but maybe Dax was... I don't think we'll ever know now.'

Tanya wiped her eyes. 'I'm never going to see him am I, Mandy? I'm never going to know who he is?' A terrible thought occurred to her, he was never going to know what had happened to her! She had no way of letting him know and he would think she'd just gone, changed her mind, left him...'

Seven o'clock. High on anticipation Matt typed in the website address, ready to click straight on Savanna's photo. He knew the site so well he even knew where her photo was on the page, almost without looking. He couldn't wait to see her in the outfit he'd chosen, she was going to look fantastic!

That's odd. He frowned, clicking on *retry*. Still nothing. He typed in the address again, making sure he had spelled it correctly and hit *enter*. Nothing. What the hell? Frantically he typed the address again and again, but nothing came up. It was gone. It couldn't be!

He typed the website name into Google and the listings came up. Yes, it was still there. But each click brought up the same results, absolutely nothing. He groaned, leaning back in his chair, running his fingers through his hair in frustration.

He didn't know what to do, felt helpless. Where was Savanna? Was she okay? What had happened to the website, had it been closed down? And most importantly, how the hell was he ever going to find her now? He knew nothing about her other than that she worked in a restaurant and bar somewhere...

'All I know is that he works in shipping,' Tanya was saying to Mandy, 'But there are shipping offices all over London and I can hardly walk into them asking for Action Man, can I? I don't know his real name, what he looks like or what he even sounds like.'

'Babes, listen to me,' Mandy hugged her, 'It was a fantasy, all part of the job hun, it wasn't real. He was probably sixty odd with a wife and ten grandchildren! Hell, maybe he was actually a woman pretending to be a man! That's the whole point, we were never supposed to know about our viewers, we were just there for their fantasies.'

Mandy paused, 'Tans, honey, I'd also connected with a nice guy, called himself *Fireman*, but that's it, we'll never chat again either. Shame really, we got on really well. But it's back to the real world for us now.'

Tanya took a deep breath. 'You're right, Mands, everything you're saying. It's just, you know, Matt and I have split permanently and I really thought I'd found someone...'

'Oh, hun, it'll all be alright in the end,' Mandy hugged her again. 'How about another drink?'

Three more drinks after that and Mandy saw Tanya safely back to her flat before saying goodnight.

'There's nothing I can do is there?' Matt was confiding in Sam, who'd called round to see if he wanted to go out for a drink. 'I'll never find her, don't know her real name, don't know where she works, that's it, it's over.'

Sam got them both another beer from the fridge. 'Maybe you had a close escape, mate, the site's obviously been closed down. You could have got caught up in whatever's happened, maybe had the cops come calling, who knows?

Maybe it's a good thing, you can get your head straight, think about sorting things out with Tanya?'

Sam felt a moment's disappointment about Nadia, pity really, he'd begun to look forward to their online chats, and to the view, if he was honest. Shame they'd never get to meet up in real life. Still, whatever had happened, he was best out of it now, and he wouldn't mention her to Matt.

'We're finished, met today, agreed to split for good.' Matt looked sadly into his beer. Sam put an arm around his shoulder consolingly. 'Too bad, mate, she was great, but your girl online was only ever a fantasy, you know that right? Whatever she told you, she was probably saying to loads of other blokes too. You need to get back out in the real world, meet a nice girl.'

Matt still thought Sam was wrong about Savanna, still believed that she'd meant everything she'd said to him, but he waved Sam off and went to bed, knowing there was nothing he could do. He'd never felt so miserable in his life. He'd lost Savanna and would never see her again...

Tanya cried herself to sleep, her outfit from Action Man still in the bag, never worn. She'd never wear it now, couldn't bear to.... couldn't bear the thought that she'd never see him again...

And that is where we leave Matt and Tanya, or perhaps, rather, Action Man and Savanna.

Their real life relationship is over and so too is their virtual one. Things could have worked out so differently for them. There are so many *what ifs?* and *if only I...*

So how about this? *What if* there is an alternative ending to this story? The choice is yours. You can end the story of lost love here, feel sorry for them and then move on with your life...

Or, you can read on for the alternative ending to this story of the lives of Matt and Tanya and their alter egos, Action Man and Savanna. The decision is yours, I hope you make the one that makes you happy...

Honey McGregor

NOW - IT'S A DATE

The day always dragged a little for Tanya when she was looking forward to her time with Action Man. It was funny, she loved her work, but- and that was when the thought struck her.

It was just the same as when she and Matt had first been together, in their early days of heady dating. When she hadn't been able to get him out of her head, had felt filled with excitement at the evening ahead. When she'd deliberated over which outfit to wear, and what to wear underneath it...

Matt yawned, wishing the day would move faster. Savanna would have received her outfit by now and would be wearing it for him tonight. A memory came, unbidden, into his head, of the time he'd surprised Tanya with a new dress for their first holiday together.

He'd spent ages going round the shops looking for the perfect sundress, picturing his beautiful girlfriend wearing it. He'd even picked up a sexy G-string for her to wear underneath it... She'd loved it, loved that he'd done that for her. And she'd looked bloody gorgeous in it too, but even more so when she'd taken it off...

Thoughts of Matt reminded Tanya that they needed to meet and talk, as agreed. She wondered if he'd also remembered that it was time, that it was nearly three months since they'd begun their trial separation.

Maybe she should text him to arrange a meeting. No, at the very least she should phone him to arrange it. She picked up her phone, just as it rang, and answered it without checking the caller ID.

'Tans?' Matt's voice registered in her ear and she found herself smiling at the sound of him after so long.

'Matt, hi, how are you?' She could hear him smiling too, as he replied that he was good. Suddenly they were both speaking at once, apologising for not having spoken before. Both laughing at how weird it was that they'd been thinking of phoning each other at the same time.

They arranged to meet the next evening, *just for a drink*, so that they could chat about everything, both of them secretly relieved that they didn't have to mention that they were busy *this* evening.

'It's a date!' Matt's voice sounded happily in her ear as she rang off. *A date.* Well of course, it was just a saying, but it still felt nice hearing him say it. She felt oddly upbeat as she worked her way through the afternoon before heading to her flat.

It's a date. Odd choice of words. Why had he said that? But still, it had felt nice saying it and, to be honest, it had felt really nice briefly chatting to Tans. It was only when his colleague asked him if he'd taken a happy pill that he realised he'd been humming and had a silly grin on his face.

SAM AND MANDY - THE DAY BEFORE

Sam was worried about his best friend, what was the right thing to do? Leave him alone to carry on his online fantasy about some girl? Or should he try to make him see sense about Tanya?

He'd known Tanya for years now, ever since she and Matt had got together, and he was really fond of her. She was a great girl, hot, funny, sexy, and perfect for Matt, why couldn't he see it?

Mandy was struggling with similar thoughts about *her* friend. She felt kind of responsible, after all, she'd got Tanya into the whole online thing. Of course, she'd never expected her to get carried away over some bloke she'd met online.

Mandy didn't know Matt, but she knew enough to know that they'd been a happy couple for years. Whatever had gone wrong between them could surely be fixed? How could Tanya just give it all up so easily, without trying at least? And whoever this guy was, online, if he even *was* a guy, well, that would never work, it was just crazy.

No, she decided, she must do something, she just needed to work out exactly what...

Sam decided to try phoning Tanya at work. At the very least he could try to talk a bit of sense into her, get her to meet up with Matt and give it another try. If she agreed he'd worry about how to get Matt to go along with it. He looked up her number and called, hoping he was doing the right thing.

Okay, Mandy decided, she'd go and talk to Tanya right now. No time like the present. She left her desk and took the lift up to the next floor, making her way to Tanya's work station.

She wasn't there, how annoying. 'She's in a meeting,' someone called out from another desk. Blast, well I'll just have to write a note and get her to call me before she goes home then, thought Mandy.

The phone on Tanya's desk started ringing and Mandy answered it automatically. 'Hi, Tanya's phone.'

The caller sounded a little caught off guard. 'Oh shit, sorry, um, d'you know when she'll be back?'

'No, can I help? That's not Matt, is it, by any chance?'

'Er, no, it's his friend, Sam. I was hoping to have a quick chat with Tanya.'

'Sam, hi!' *This could work.* 'I'm Mandy, Tanya's friend. 'You wouldn't happen to be a *close* friend of Matt's would you?'

A few minutes of chatting and they'd discovered they were both thinking along the same lines. Neither mentioned the online complication, for obvious reasons.

'Listen,' said Sam, 'How about we meet up for a proper chat then, see if we can come up with a plan?' She sounded nice, *really* nice, he'd be more than happy meeting her for a drink to talk about their friends' problems.

'Okay, sure.' Mandy smiled to herself, he sounded cute, she didn't mind meeting him at all... and all for a good cause...

Sam walked into the bar, scanning the faces, looking for Mandy. 'I'll be the hot brunette propping up the bar,' she'd joked.

He stopped in his tracks, taking in the, well, yes, the hot brunette. She was stunning, gorgeous.

She turned to face him and her face broke into a big smile. 'Sam?'

Oh my God. What a total hunk. This was going to be an extremely enjoyable meeting...

Two hours later, and a few drinks later, much had been discussed. Plans had been agreed and set in place and they were both feeling very pleased with themselves.

They were now sitting very close together, well, the pub *had* filled up, and they'd been *more* than happy to squash up together on a small banquette. The attraction was definitely mutual, although neither one had acknowledged it to the other. It was time for one of them to make a move.

'Fancy a bite to eat?' Sam took charge. Without hesitation Mandy agreed and they left the pub for a small restaurant just along the road.

Mandy was having a blast. Sam was so funny, she'd not this much fun in ages. She fleetingly thought of the guy she'd been chatting to online, her *Fireman*, he was also very funny. But nothing could beat being with a real person, especially when he was as gorgeous as Sam.

Sam couldn't believe his luck. Mandy was a total babe, hot as hell and such a great sense of humour. She reminded him, a little, of that hot chick online, Nadia, there was something about her... No, Mandy was way hotter, and she was real, right here with him. He was falling for her, he could feel it...

The evening ended very pleasurably, outside Mandy's flat. No need to rush things, they'd be seeing each other again real soon.

Without knowing it, each had made a decision. No more *Watch Me Want Me*, for Sam and no more part-time work at *Watch Me Want Me*, for Mandy.

Now they just had to execute their plan together...

Matt kept coming into her mind as she showered and prepared for her evening ahead. She slipped on her favourite sundress, remembering as she did so that it was the one Matt had brought her all those years ago, for their first holiday together. On a whim, she rummaged through her underwear drawer, finding the G-string he'd bought her too. It was a little faded but she slipped it on.

Strange. Why had she chosen to wear the dress and G-string tonight, she wondered to herself? Was it her subconscious trying to tell her something? Doubts began to creep in about what she'd been doing as Savanna.

Savanna wasn't real. Action Man wasn't real. They were two people pretending to be other people. Had she been fooling herself? Matt was real. She'd loved him and he'd loved her. Maybe they could love each other properly again, if they tried...

She picked up the bag, with the gorgeous outfit Action Man had chosen for her, and placed her blonde wig inside with it. She was ready to go, so why was she hesitating?

After his shower Matt pulled on long shorts and a tee, adding a shirt over it. As he checked himself in the mirror, he realised he'd chosen a shirt that Tanya had bought him for one of his birthdays. He realised that she'd been in the back of his mind ever since they'd spoken earlier.

He paused, thinking about Tanya. Was he about to throw away the best thing that had ever happened to him in his life? They'd been happy, really happy. What had gone wrong other than that they'd stopped trying?

What if they were to try again? Was he really going to choose a girl he'd met on a sex site over Tanya? Tanya was real. Savanna wasn't real, she was acting. As he pondered these confused thoughts his front doorbell rang and he went to answer it.

What am I doing? Tanya was still standing in the hallway of the flat. She felt confused. Her doorbell rang and she answered it in a bit of a daze.

'Mandy! What are you doing here?' She smiled in surprise as Mandy took her arm. 'What's going on?'

'Sorry, Tans honey, but you're coming with me!' Mandy refused to tell her anything, just held onto her arm tightly as she led her from her flat and put her in the car. She drove them in silence, refusing to answer her questions apart from to say that she was doing what she should have done a long time ago.

Tanya's head was spinning, she was supposed to be on her way to work. Sh was supposed to be preparing for Action Man. But something made her, too stay silent.

'Sam! Alright, mate? What's happening? Mark? Nick? What's going on, guys get off me!' His friends held him firmly as they frogmarched him to the car and pushed him in the back, Mark and Nick getting in either side of him so ther was no escape.

'Call it an intervention, call it what you like, Matt, but I should have done thi a long time ago,' Sam said, as he drove them off.

An intervention? What the fuck? What was his crazy mate going on about He was supposed to be going online soon, to see Savanna. But then he though about his hesitation earlier, had he definitely been planning to go through with it all?

Mandy hustled Tanya into the pub and led her straight through to the restaurant section, nodding at the waitress, who didn't seem at all surprised by their arrival.

As Tanya sat down, bemused, wondering if she and Mandy were going to have dinner for some unexplained reason, she looked up, her eyes widening in surprise. There was Matt! And Sam, Mark and Nick!

Sam was holding Matt's arm, steering him past the same unfazed waitress the two other guys hovering as if on guard. Matt was pushed unceremoniousl down into the chair opposite her, looking as confused as she was.

A quick peck on Tanya's cheek from Sam, with a 'You look gorgeous, babes! and the couple were left alone.

They were somewhat bemused to hear Sam saying 'And you look particularly gorgeous, babes,' to Mandy, as she giggled, before they hugged each other and walked out, arms wrapped around each other.

Matt and Tanya looked at each other in absolute astonishment. They began to laugh as they both spoke at the same time. 'Did you know anything about this, or about them?' Shaking their heads, they both confessed to having had no idea.

Thoughts of everything else went out of their minds as they looked at each other, remembering each other's features, their smiles, both thinking how great it was to see each other.

They started talking, rushing over their words as they found so much to say all of a sudden. The hovering waitress gave them pause, asking them if they wanted something to drink, and Matt's quick look at her and 'Bottle of our favourite?' gave Tanya a warm feeling inside as she nodded her agreement.

As they sipped their wine, they looked at each other over their glasses.

'You look gorgeous Tans, you really do. Don't I recognise that dress?' Matt's eyes flashed at her with a teasing glint in them.

She flushed, feeling pleased. 'You too, Matt, and I think I've seen that shirt before haven't I?'

They were flirting, the same thought occurred to them both.

'You always knew what would suit me, Tans.' Matt reached over the table, taking her other hand in his and stroking it gently. She kept her hand in his, loving his touch, feeling butterflies softly fluttering in her stomach.

'Oh, Matt,' she groaned, 'What have we been doing?' Her eyes looked up at him, feeling sad at how much time they'd wasted apart.

'Wasting time,' he whispered, lifting her hand to his lips and kissing it gently. He loved her! Suddenly he realised it so clearly, he felt it with every bone in his body.

I still love him as much as ever! The thought jolted through her body as she leaned over the table towards him and they kissed slowly.

The waitress's cough brought them back to the real world and they looked at each other enquiringly.

'Shall we order something to eat? Do you have to be anywhere?' Matt looked at her anxiously.

'No,' she said, with a smile, and a sudden realisation, 'I think here is exactly where I'm supposed to be...'

Matt was pleased, this was exactly where he needed to be too, he realised happily.

The evening was fabulous. They talked, reminisced, laughed and flirted and both wanted it to go on forever. But both of them also knew that they were keeping certain things from each other...

By mutual agreement they headed to their house after dinner, which, as Matt pointed out correctly, was still *their* house. Matt opened another bottle of wine and poured them both a glass, sitting on the couch beside Tanya.

Nerves and awkwardness suddenly kicked in, on both sides.

I need to tell him, thought Tanya, I have to tell him I was unfaithful, I'll never feel comfortable keeping a secret from him...

Fuck, I'm going to have to confess, thought Matt, we can't start over if I'm keeping a secret from her...

They both started talking at the same time.

'Matt, I need to tell you something...' Tanya looked up at Matt, her eyes anxious.

'Tans, I must just tell you something...' Matt's worried eyes looked into hers.

They moved apart slightly, still holding hands, both realising they had things to confess. As they looked into each other's eyes they each tried to find the words, wondering just how much they needed to tell.

'Did you sleep with someone else?' Tanya's voice was a whisper, as she dreaded his reply.

63

'No,' relief flooded through Matt, he could honestly say he hadn't slept with anyone else. 'I didn't sleep with anyone, Tans, I promise you.' He paused, how could he put it without it sounding too bad? 'But I did kind of meet someone and we talked a lot. But that's all, I never even touched her, I promise you. But you? Did you meet someone? Did you sleep with him? I want to kill him!'

Tanya felt massive relief, she hadn't actually *slept* with him, had she? Thank God! 'No, I promise you, Matt, I also kind of met someone, but I didn't sleep with him. We just talked, shared things, you know. We never even touched either, that's the truth.' Well, it *was* the truth, she was just leaving quite a bit out, but when it came down to it, she'd never even met the guy, it had never been a real relationship.

'Then that's all I need to know, Tans, nothing more.' Slight guilt was making him feel generous. 'We both turned to other people to fill the void, that's all right?'

She nodded, her own guilt making her want to move on and grant them both forgiveness for whatever and whoever they'd shared their time with, while they'd been apart.

'Oh, Matt, we'd just stopped making the effort with each other. We'd stopped talking, we didn't have fun anymore, we didn't make any effort with each other. The person I... talked to... was just someone to share with, we never so much as kissed.'

God, he was so relieved, everything was going to be alright! 'Me too! She was just someone I could talk to about my day, she showed interest in me, made me feel interesting. You're right, we'd stopped trying, stopped making an effort with each other, that's all. And I promise you I never laid a hand on her, and I never kissed her.'

'So maybe our trial separation was good for us in the end?' She looked at him enquiringly. 'Can we move on, forget about all of this, start again?'

Matt's answer was to take her in his arms and their bodies came together naturally, familiarity lending extra pleasure to the experience, as slowly they kissed and touched each other.

Desire took them over and they couldn't stop, their movements becoming more frantic as they removed their clothing. 'I've seen these panties before haven't I?' asked Matt, grinning, as he tantalisingly pulled them down her legs and dropped them onto the floor...

Seeing Matt's naked body again after so long filled her with longing. She ran her hands over every inch of his flesh, remembering how good he felt. His cock was hard as she held it, lowering herself to take him in her mouth.

Tanya's body looked amazing! Matt was hard as a rock and couldn't stop drinking in the sight of her, naked and beautiful. She was sexier than ever as she straddled him, caressing his body with a new-found confidence. His hands roamed over her breasts before moving lower to caress her hips and thighs, loving the feel of her smooth skin under them.

He buried his face in her breasts, kissing her nipples and sucking them hungrily, before groaning as she moved lower to take him in her mouth. He wanted to devour every part of her and he swung her over onto the couch, parting her legs to take his first, remembered, taste of her sweetness.

She writhed with pleasure as Matt's lips found her hot desire between her legs, running her hands through his hair as he sucked her, until she moaned out loud, pushing herself against him and wanting his tongue to push deep inside her.

He sucked and probed her wet pussy with his tongue, his hands reaching under her buttocks to gently part them. She was so wet, his fingers slipped easily into every part of her as she groaned out loud. His cock was leaking cum, as she began to grind her mound into his face, and he lifted himself up to enter her, locking eyes with her as they began to move together.

Tanya gripped Matt's buttocks to pull him deeper inside her as they neared orgasm, both not wanting it to end but unable to stop themselves.

They gave themselves up to the sheer pleasure of their union, their time apart, and everything that had happened completely forgotten as, in one perfect moment they came together, crying out and holding each other tightly, trying to squeeze every last drop of pleasure from each other.

They were so happy these days, walking on air! Tanya was back in the house and they'd celebrated with a dinner party, inviting their friends as a way of thanking them for their part in the reunion.

Tanya and Mandy had a quick chat up in the bedroom later that evening. 'We'll never mention it again,' Mandy reassured her, 'It's all over, finished, you didn't actually cheat with anyone, you didn't sleep with anyone else, did you? I'm just so pleased that you're happy!'

Matt and Sam had their own little chat in the kitchen. 'Forget about it, mate, I'll never mention the website, your secret's safe with me! It's not as if you actually slept with any of the chicks, did you? So, you didn't actually cheat on Tans with anyone, not really. You've made the right choice, Tans is right for you, I'm happy for you!'

Of course, they each had their moments where a memory came unbidden into one of their minds. For Matt it might be an advert for a sex site, but he resisted the temptation to even look. He certainly didn't need it, not with his and Tanya's amazing sex life these days.

Did he think of Savanna at all? Did he feel guilty about dropping her without a word? Yes, if he was honest, but he gradually convinced himself that she had been acting a role, something she must have done with many other guys online.

He'd had a narrow escape. He'd nearly lost Tanya forever over a girl on a sex site and he'd never make the same mistake again.

And Tanya, did she think of her Action Man? Well, for one thing, Matt paid her so much attention and their sex life was so good again that she certainly wasn't feeling frustrated any more. She made more effort with her appearance and the clothes she wore, which sometimes reminded her of getting ready for her work at *Watch Me Want Me*.

This would, of course, bring back a memory of their chats and the other things they'd done... But she realised now how close she'd come to losing Matt over an unknown person online. Whoever he was, he had probably had loads of girls online. If anything, she'd probably had a narrow escape...

Tanya was keeping *one* secret from Matt though... the bag was hidden right at the back of her closet... Well, come on, she said to herself, the outfit was too gorgeous to throw away and the wig was so stunning...

Matt's birthday was coming up in a couple of days and suddenly she knew *exactly* how she was going to surprise him...

The day came and Tanya set the scene, champagne and glasses laid out ready, a note left for him to read as he got home from work. She then prepared herself, filled with excited anticipation...

Matt picked up the note and read it with interest. Hello, Tans had organised him a birthday surprise... He wasn't allowed in the bedroom, she'd placed his clothes in the spare room. He was to shower and dress and then find his surprise in their bedroom. This was going to be good, he could tell...

She lay back on the bed waiting for him, excitement driving her crazy. He was going to love it, she just knew! She was feeling hot just thinking about what they were going to do together. She looked down at herself, stretching out sexily so that the dress fell open a little to reveal the tops of her stocking clad legs...

She watched through half-closed eyes as she heard him open the door...

He gasped in shock. 'Savanna?' What the fuck? How could it be? What was happening? Where was Tans? 'What are you... Where's... You're wearing the outfit! What the hell's happening?'

Tanya heard Matt gasp and then say *that* name... *her* name... and mention the outfit, that only Action Man could have known about... God no, please no...

But one look at his face and she knew. He was white with shock and she looked at him in horror as they both realised the truth. 'You,' Tanya stammered, 'You're Action Man... Oh my God...' She sat up, trembling.

'And you're Savanna... God, Tans, I can't believe it...' Matt sat down on the bed, still in shock. His eyes ran over Tanya in the outfit he'd chosen for Savanna, and over the wig, that beautiful platinum blonde hair...

They sat there in stunned silence, each trying to process what they now knew. They knew *everything*, what they'd said to each other online, what they'd shared, what they'd *done*...

66

Suddenly he grinned, fuck it, he couldn't help it. 'You look bloody hot in the outfit I chose though!'

Tanya grinned too, taking his hand, it was all going to be alright. 'It's gorgeous, I love it! But, oh, Matt, what now? How do we get through this? I'm not sure I can bear you knowing what I did...' She looked at him anxiously.

He took her other hand and looked into her eyes. 'Tans,' he said softly, 'I did it too... we both did. But at least we did it together. Think about it, we found each other even when we were apart...'

'Like we were always meant to be together...' whispered Tanya, as he nodded, smiling at her.

As they looked at each other they felt the heat rising between them and shifted slightly, a mutual look giving tacit agreement to what was going to happen...

Suddenly they were transported, he to watching Savanna on his screen, and she to being *live* in her room, knowing that Action Man was watching her, telling her what to do...

'Lean back,' he whispered, 'Open your legs for me... I want to see what you're not wearing underneath that dress...' He watched, heavy with desire, as her dress fell open to reveal her pussy, for his eyes only. His cock hardened painfully and he had to resist the urge to take it out and hold it, he wasn't sitting at his laptop now...

She did as he asked, her instant arousal causing her to fill with a hot wetness between her legs. 'Do you like that?' she asked, as she spread her legs further.

'I love it.' He groaned, trying to resist the urge to touch her just yet. 'Pull your top down, I want to see what's underneath.'

Hot with desire, she pulled the top of her dress bodice down, revealing the lace bustier supporting her swelling breasts. She reached out to him, undoing a button on his shirt. 'Take your shirt off,' she whispered.

He ripped his shirt off, unable to tear his eyes away from the sight of her perfect breasts, their nipples teasingly peeking above the lace. He reached out a hand and touched the jutting pink buds so that she gasped. His cock was leaking into his shorts and he undid them, letting it spring free.

Slowly he pulled her bustier down and buried his face in her breasts, groaning at how he'd imagined doing this so many times with Savanna. As he reached between her legs, he felt her take his cock, squeezing it gently as she moved her hand up and down its length.

She didn't know if she was Tanya, or Savanna, and she didn't care anymore, she felt like she was in a dream world of desire, barely able to control herself. The feel of his hand between her legs was too good... she was too wet... She opened her legs wider...

Matt lifted himself up to kiss her on her lips, sliding his tongue between them to curl hungrily with hers, before slowly trailing his mouth down her body. This

had been his fantasy... Who *was* he right now? Was he Matt? Or was he Actio
Man? And did it matter anyway...

His tongue trailed tantalisingly over her exposed mound and flicked gentl
over her swollen labia so that they opened like a flower, revealing her clit, in al
its engorged desire. He could hear her moaning, her body wriggling underneatl
him impatiently, as she creamed into his mouth.

Tanya pushed herself against his mouth, wanting his tongue, wanting him t
suck everything from her. She was crazy with heated desire as she started t
come, her body shuddering upwards in spasms as her orgasm took over and sh
cried out in gasps, not wanting it to end.

'Fuck me!' she cried out, pulling on his shoulders so that he moved up he
body and, needing no further invitation, rammed his cock inside her urgent hot
creamy, wetness.

She was still coming, waves rushing over her, as he began to thrust dee
inside her, his arms wrapped tightly around her. He couldn't hold it, he
spasming tightness felt too good, and he came in a torrent, filling her up so ful
that his cum overflowed, its sticky wetness slicking over their thighs, as thei
bodies stayed pressed hard against each other. Gasping, they slumped togethe
on the bed.

They stayed there, holding each other, as their breathing slowly returned t
normal, whispering how much they loved each other. Neither of them were sur
who they'd just been, which couple had actually been making love...

The only thing they were sure of was that all their fantasies had come true
in real life... and that they could have them as many times as they wanted to
They could have them forever, because they were exactly where they wer
supposed to be...

THANK YOU

Thanks for reading my story, I hope you enjoyed it! I'd love it if you could leave a few words in a review on Amazon, so that others can read about my books.

Want to read more from Honey McGregor?
Choose from Private Pleasures: The Collection and Dina Island – a novella.

Private Pleasures: The Collection is an anthology of nine erotic fantasies, ranging from playing away to role play, from steamy seductions to total sexual submission... Great stories, something for your every mood, Honey McGregor's stories are the perfect escape into a world of sexual desire and fulfilment. Close the door, lower the blind, and find pleasure at your fingertips... Private Pleasures is Honey's most popular book - a top bestseller, a top most-wanted, and top most-gifted, book for erotica fans.

Dina Island is a sexy island escape with gently erotic scenes. As Racquel holidays in private island luxury and finds herself attracted to Anthony, her host, Honey McGregor takes you on a sensual journey of sexual reawakening and voyeurism. Gentle seduction and eroticism - a sexy beach read, or weekend read, to get you hot and bothered, and much more, and make you wish you were there.

Here's how you can stay in touch with Honey McGregor:

www.facebook.com/honeymcgregorauthor
honeymcgregor.blogspot.com

Until the next time... the pleasure's been all mine... and hopefully yours too...
Honey McGregor